A Troublesome Inheritance

Brian Peters

Published by New Generation Publishing in 2017

Cover design by Jacqueline Abromeit

ISBN: 978-1-78719-407-6

www.newgeneration-publishing.com

Also by this author

Kidnap Under A Suffolk Sky 978-1-78719-408-3
2017

The Reluctant Samaritan
978-1-78719-409-0
2017

The Spiral Steps
978-1-78003-858-2
2015

The Silver Box
978-1-90562-156-9
2007

To my lovely wife, Heather

THE FUNERAL

Asil Daniels strode purposefully along the tarmac path towards the church, dressed soberly in a smart navy business suit over a crisp white blouse. She looked older than her 19 years. Her face, framed by her dark hair, was pale and drawn.

It was a quarter to 11 on a warm June morning, the sun danced through the trees that lined the path. She spotted the diminutive figure of Mahari Artaxis, her deceased uncle's friend, facing towards her away from the other mourners. Waiting expectantly, he recognized her as she drew nearer. He raised both arms slowly sideways to shoulder height then let them drop to his side in a gesture of helplessness. Asil quickened her pace and, reaching him, embraced his small frame and felt his body begin to convulse in silent sobs. She couldn't contain her emotions any longer and felt a tear run down her cheek and nestle in his curly black hair. She composed herself and after a few seconds pushed him gently away to arm's length, then wiped the tears from his eyes with her thumbs.

"My poor, dear Mahari. Come on, we must be brave now. Let's go inside and pay our last respects."

He looked up at her and nodded, turned, and then took her hand, child-like, and they joined the congregation that already filled the church.

Mahari Artaxis was 24 years old, a tiny 4' 6" tall but well proportioned, with the build of an athlete. A shock of wavy black hair framed a tanned complexion that betrayed his Turkish origin. Mahari was born into a very poor family, the second of seven children, in Eregli on the east coast of northern Turkey. His early childhood was spent wearing ragged clothes handed down from his elder brothers. At four years old he suffered a problem with his hearing and became profoundly deaf. His father was killed in an accident working on the railway when Mahari was seven and from then on he had to scavenge for food, steal it if he could, and rummage through rubbish tips for anything useable in the home or that could be repaired and sold. He and his elder brother were always the ones on whom the burden of providing for the family fell. Even at this age it was obvious that he was smaller than his peers. To avoid being bullied at school he developed a knack of performing, doing double somersaults, walking on his hands and diving off the high rocks into the sea near his home to amuse the other children.

A travelling circus came to town when he was nine. The jugglers, tightrope walkers and clowns fascinated him, and every night of the week he would sneak under the canvas big top to watch. On the sixth night he was caught by Stefan, one of the staff, and taken to the manager, who occupied a large caravan next to the big top. Carried in squirming frantically he was dumped on the floor in front of the manager's desk. The manager smiled and raised his eyebrows to Stefan for an explanation.

"I've watched him every night this week Mr Kezman, sneaking in under the canvas. He's been entertaining the other kids in the queue outside with acrobatics. He's good and I thought maybe we could use him." Stefan looked down at Mahari and smiled at him.

He interpreted the men's smiles as friendly and decided to show them just what he could do. He jumped up off the floor and did his double somersault, back-flips and walked across the floor on his hands. He stood up, hands on hips and beamed at the manager.

"Well, little one, where did you learn such tricks?" said Mr Kezman. Mahari watched Mr Kezman's mouth intently as he spoke but couldn't lip-read well enough to decipher what had been said to him. So he pointed to his ears, then his mouth, then held his hands out, palms up, and shrugged. The manager looked at Stefan, then back at Mahari.

"Do you think his family would let him join the circus if we could use him?" said Stefan, who had taken an instant liking to this cheeky young child.

Kezman thought for a few seconds, nodded approval and said, "But can you read and write, little one?" while making writing movements with his hand. Mahari understood, nodded furiously and ran to the desk. He picked up a pencil and wrote his name, Mahari Artaxis, and his address on a piece of paper, handed it to the manager and pointed to himself, chest thrust out and smiling broadly. Kezman laughed out loud. "Well, Mahari, let's see what your parents have to say about this." He turned to Stefan. "Stefan, take this young man home and talk to his parents. Tell them we'll provide his keep and send money once a month for a year. If he doesn't make the grade, we'll send him home again."

Stefan immediately grasped Mahari's hand, pulled him out of the caravan and led him to his home.

His mother cried when Stefan put the proposition to her. She loved Mahari, but desperately needed some money to feed the other children – and Mahari would be one less mouth to feed if she agreed to let him go. She also realised that he wanted to join the circus more than anything in the world. She hugged Mahari to her breast and ran her fingers through his hair, tears streaming down her cheeks. His mother had learned sign language and Mahari had been a quick learner from an early age. "Go, my son if it's want you want. Promise to write to me, and tell me if they don't look after you properly, won't you?"

He stayed with the circus for many years, travelling all over Europe. Greece, Hungary, Germany, France, Italy – too many countries to remember. He had learned all sorts of skills – trapeze, horse riding, conjuring, being a clown. He grew strong and his sunny disposition made him popular with the other performers. During the first few months he got his colleagues to write home for him. But the letters gradually dried up and he could receive no replies because the circus was constantly on the move. It was in Budapest, when things went badly wrong. He fell from a horse he was riding bareback and fractured his right leg in two places. The manager took him to the local hospital and left him there to recover. When the circus moved on, the surgeon insisted that Mahari be left to recover fully. The break didn't heal, and the leg had to be broken again and re-set. Weeks turned into months before he fully recovered. Eventually, the hospital had to discharge him. Not a word had been heard from the circus and no one knew where it had gone, and he had no means of finding out. Mahari was left with nowhere to live, no money and no friends. He got less active and was reduced to begging in the street and sleeping wherever he could lay his head, covering himself with newspapers during the cold nights and scavenging by day for food.

Gordon Bancroft was running a surgery in Budapest at the time. He passed Mahari's pitch on the main road where he was begging on a few occasions. His plight intrigued him. He stopped and spoke to Mahari, then, realising his impediments, encouraged him to write down how it was that he came to be in this predicament. Mahari was delighted when Bancroft offered to take him to the surgery. The doctor soon got him back to health and fitness. He arranged for Mahari to accompany him back to England when his time at the surgery came to an end, describing him on the entry paperwork as his manservant.

He had remained with the doctor ever since. A couple of years ago Doctor Bancroft had funded an operation involving an implant that had partially restored Mahari's hearing.

After the service many of the people that she knew offered Asil their condolences, none more warmly than John Nolloth, the private detective who had been largely responsible for saving her when she was kidnapped eight years ago. He looked fit and well and certainly appeared a lot younger than his 64 years. The Reverend Anthony O'Malley kept Asil in conversation for a long time. He had provided refuge at the Old Rectory when Asil was ten years old and was being been pursued prior to her abduction. He'd not seen Asil since she'd moved to Suffolk a year previously, and he was anxious to know how she was settling down there. But his main concern was her state of mind following the death of Gordon Bancroft, and to provide any solace that was in his power. Asil had the highest regard for Anthony, but any religious beliefs she might have held had been destroyed by the untimely death of her parents at the hands of her insane aunt Morag. Her friend, Doctor Bancroft, whom she called Uncle, had been her mentor and father figure since then, and she was going to miss him terribly. He had always been there for her, offering help and advice whenever she had needed it.

Asil drove Mahari to the cemetery, following the hearse and the other funeral cars.

"What will you do now?" she asked as they walked in the grounds after the burial, admiring the many floral tributes. He shook his head, staring at the ground, and shrugged his shoulders. Asil stopped and turned to face him. She took his face in her hands and looked down into his sad eyes.

"You *must* come and stay with me until the will is settled. You'll always have a home with me no matter what, my lovely little man." She smiled down at him and kissed him on the forehead. He squeezed her hand and nodded vigorously.

"Look, tomorrow, shall we pack your things and drive down to my home in Suffolk? Mrs Wade will be delighted to have you stay and so will Belynda; it's been far too long since they've seen you and I can't bear to think of you alone in that big, dark house. She'll prepare a room for you and feed you up until you're back to your old self." He nodded enthusiastically, and smiled. She put her arms around him, hugged him and laughed, enjoying the first positives of that sad day.

The doctor's death had been sudden and unexpected. His health had been good for an 80 year old, although he used a walking stick due to an arthritic knee. He was tall, slim, active and cheerful, until struck down by a massive heart attack ten days previously. His death had come as a huge shock to Asil and Mahari. Gordon Bancroft had steered her through the tragedy of the death of her parents, her ill treatment and abduction by her mad aunt Morag, and again when two Romanians had kidnapped her two years later when trying to get access to the treasure. That inheritance, though gained by her father in extremely dubious circumstances, had been overseen and managed by her uncle and put into trust until she reached the age of 21. It had provided ample funds for her to buy, and move into, a large five-bedroom house in Suffolk a year ago. She chose Suffolk for two reasons. Doctor Bancroft had found her a safe house in Thorpeness on the Suffolk coast at the time when she was being pursued. She fell in love with the big East Anglian skies and the bracing air. And it was a very long way from Wales, the scene of so many bad memories for her. She remembered playing on the beach with her Springer spaniel, Patch, sailing on the Mere, fish and chips and cream teas in Aldeburgh, eating out in the garden on long summer evenings.

She had persuaded Mrs Wade, whom she had lived with since Aunt Morag had been put away, to come and stay with her as a live-in housekeeper, bringing Belynda, her daughter, with her. Asil and Belynda, although good friends, had grown apart socially since reaching their teens and lived entirely separate lives in spite of being the same age.

The value of the inheritance that her father had secured from Romania was almost beyond her imagination. She had ambiguous feelings about it. She loved her father dearly but couldn't bring herself to think of him as having been guilty of stealing this hoard of treasure. However, she had learned from Mr Kurasowa, her father's Japanese friend, that he had very little choice in the matter. Apparently, while working for the Foreign Office in Romania, a leading politician had asked him to look after this treasure trove until the political situation had improved, as he was fearful that it would be taken from him. So her father had been merely a temporary custodian. Unfortunately, the situation worsened, the politician disappeared along with his entire family after a coupe and was never heard of again. Bill Daniels, rightly or wrongly, kept quiet about the treasure and took steps to prevent it ever falling into the hands of the corrupt government that had undoubtedly murdered his friend the politician. He had Kurosawa construct an electronic device in the guise of a silver box that contained the key to the whereabouts of the treasure. Bill Daniels had not even told his wife Carole about it. However, he did entrust this information, together with the silver box, to Gordon Bancroft, knowing that he would ensure Asil's best interest should anything untoward happen to him. Fortunately he had made a will before the tragic premature deaths of both himself and his wife Carole..

The sale of only three of the paintings, all by famous artists, had realised close to a million pounds, part of which had been used to buy the house in Suffolk and to furnish it. The rest of the paintings, gold and silver artefacts, figurines, ceramics, clocks and watches and various other trinkets were all deposited in a bank vault and had been catalogued and valued at close on three million pounds. Asil had been granted an annual allowance by Doctor Bancroft until her 21st birthday. But now, what would happen after his death was uncertain, both for Asil and Mahari.

The reading of the will was to be in a couple of week's time. Two weeks of uncertainty lay ahead for both of them.

Asil was oblivious to the fact that the news of her uncle's death had reached across the continent to Romania from where those valuable artefacts had originated. A series of illicit films had been made 15 years previously at a number of parties held at a rich industrialist's country mansion. Several high profile and influential people, some in the present government, some in important positions in business and some in show business, had featured in highly embarrassing circumstances. Should any of these films come to the public's attention, the stability of the present government would be severely threatened. One person, very high up in the security service now, had been involved at the time and had taken it upon himself to find out what had happened to those films. It had taken him three years to discover that they had left the country and were now in England. Without disclosing any of this information to anyone else in government circles, he had set in motion plans to retrieve these very films. He recruited a man that he knew would be discreet, who would be ruthless in carrying out his task and would be totally reliable. His name was Ion Campeanu.

Campeanu was at this very moment watching proceedings at the funeral whilst a colleague of his was staying in Suffolk, his task being to keep watch on Asil's house and survey its surroundings.

HOME

After the wake, held in a rather stark local hotel conference room, Asil drove Mahari back to the doctor's house. She realised that he didn't want to stay in the house a moment longer than necessary. He wandered about the rooms aimlessly, looking forlorn, picking up various objects, looking at them and putting them down again with a sigh. Asil watched him in despair until she could bear it no longer and stopped him in the kitchen.

"Mahari, shall we go straight back to Suffolk today? What do you think?"

He looked up at her and thought for a moment, then smiled broadly at her and nodded approval enthusiastically.

"Then that's what we'll do. I'll get my things together. If we leave in a couple of hours we could be back home by about eight or nine this evening if we're lucky with the traffic. I'll ring Mrs Wade right now and let her know that I'm coming back a day early and bringing a visitor with me!"

Mahari hurried to his bedroom and immediately started to pack an overnight bag. They set about making the house secure before leaving.

After an uneventful and boring motorway drive from Wales, it was a pleasure to enter rural Suffolk. The late afternoon sunshine brought out the beauty of the blossoming shrubs, trees and hedgerows along the country roads that could be justly defined as sylvan; not that Mahari noticed as he had fallen fast asleep once on the move. They reached the village of Monks Eleigh at 7.30 that evening. Asil pulled the car into the driveway of her large modern house and drove up to the front door, the tyres scrunching loudly on the gravel. As the car stopped, Mahari woke up, stretched, wiped the sleep from his eyes and took in the view of the house. His eyes widened in surprise at the size of it.

Mrs Wade appeared at the door and greeted them both as they disembarked, all smiles and rushing to hug Mahari while Belynda did the same to Asil. A smell of cooking wafted out of the open door. Asil thought she recognised it as one of Mrs Wade's renowned steak and kidney pies, at least she hoped that it was.

Marjorie Wade insisted on hearing all about the funeral; who was there, what the service was like, how many floral tributes were there and whom they were from, how the Reverend Anthony O'Malley was, etc. She took Mahari up to see his room and unpack. He was delighted to have a room upstairs, full of light, and with a view of the garden. It was very different from living in the rather gloomy underground house with Doctor Bancroft.

After thoroughly enjoying the meal, Mrs Wade's appetite for knowledge of the funeral and the people she knew in Towyn was still insatiable. Asil tried to supply her with all the information that she could, but she and Mahari were both exhausted, not surprising after their eventful day, and to Mrs Wade's disappointment they made their excuses and retired early.

****

A silver Mercedes joined a large dark coloured Audi saloon, parked a hundred yards along the lane from the house. A man got out and walked to the Audi, opened the passenger door and joined the driver. Through binoculars they could ascertain that there was a burglar alarm box fitted high on the front wall of the house and that there were security lights on the one side that they could see and one above the front door.

They waited well into the evening and noted the time that bedroom lights were turned on, in which rooms and the time that the downstairs lights were extinguished. Only then did they return to their hotel in Hintlesham, five miles to the south.

****

Although Asil had lived in the village for a year now, she didn't know any of the locals well, just a nod and exchange of greetings. Being away during the week working for the head office of a charity in Ipswich made socializing difficult at weekends. Not much occurred in Monks Eleigh that interested her unfortunately. As for making friends at the office, most of the others were part-timers and a generation older than she. Oh, they were very friendly, but she had very little in common with them, and apart from agreeing to go to tea with a couple of them at various times, she kept them at a distance and never talked about her past.

She had made an acquaintance with a local man, Luke Lomax.

Luke was aware that a very attractive young lady had moved into the village. He had assumed that Mrs Wade was her mother and that Belynda was her sister. But village gossip gained by his mother had soon established that it was Miss Daniels that had purchased the house and that Mrs Wade was the housekeeper and that Belynda was Mrs Wade's daughter. This intrigued him and added an air of mystery as to how this had come about. Why would an ostensibly wealthy young and attractive girl come to live in a small village like Monks Eleigh?

He had helped fix Asil's car one wet Friday evening when it had suffered a puncture not far from her house. She had been returning home from visiting a work colleague who hadn't been well. It was about ten o'clock, dark and humid. The sky was still leaden with rain clouds and the wet tarmac shone black in her headlights. She was just a few hundred yards from home when her front tyre suffered a blow-out. It nearly wrenched the steering wheel out of her hands. Asil stopped, got out and saw that her front offside tyre was absolutely flat, the rim of the wheel resting on the road. *Why does this always happen when it's raining?* she thought. But fortunately it was close to the house.

A car coming from the opposite direction pulled up next to her. The man opened his window.

"Do you need any help?" he asked.

"It's OK, I only live just up the road. Do you think I can drive it a little way like this?"

He looked down at the shredded tyre and shook his head.

"No chance," he said, rolled his window up and started to drive off. Asil placed her hands on her hips and was about to say something rude when the car stopped and then reversed to her side of the road. The man got out and walked to the boot of her car.

"I presume you've got a spare? Is the boot unlocked?"

"Yes, of course, but…"

Without being asked, he opened the boot, lifted the carpet and pulled out the tool kit and jack.

"It's only an emergency wheel, so you won't be able to drive far on it, but it'll get you home alright."

He jacked up the car, removed the wheel and fitted the spare while Asil looked on feeling helpless. He was getting very wet in what was now a light drizzle and so was she.

"There you go, didn't take long, did it?" he said smiling. She noted how good looking he was and what nice eyes he had.

"I can't thank you enough, that's really kind of you. Look, you must come home and clean up and get yourself dry. It's only just a couple of hundred yards. Follow me, OK?"

She didn't give him a chance to say no.

She got in the car and started it up and waited for him to turn round which she was pleased to see that he did. When she got into the house, she was pleased that Mrs Wade and Belynda were both in bed.

"Come in, please. I'm sorry, I don't know your name?"

"It's Luke, Luke Lomax."

"Well Luke, my knight in shining armour! The cloakroom's there if you'd like to clean up. I'll make us a cup of tea, shall I, or would you rather have coffee?"

She was amused to see that he blushed.

"No, tea will be fine, white no sugar please."

He came out of the cloakroom and stood by an armchair while Asil was in the kitchen She emerged with a tray of tea and biscuits.

"For goodness sake sit down, Luke! I do hope you won't get into trouble for being late home. Do you live far away?"

He deliberately hadn't let on that he only lived a stone's throw from her house. When he revealed the fact, she laughed and accused him of being less than honest with her. He blushed again and confessed that he'd been enjoying her company too much.

Asil was a bit annoyed when Mrs Wade appeared in her dressing gown, immediately embarrassed to find a stranger in the room.

"Oh, I'm so sorry Asil, I just thought…"

"It's alright Auntie, this kind man helped me change a tyre just up the road, and so the least I could do was offer him a cup of tea."

"It's Mr Lomax isn't it?" Mrs Wade said.

"That's right," he said, even more embarrassed.

"Well, I'll say goodnight to you both. Sorry to intrude." She went back upstairs to bed.

They both giggled to each other like naughty children when she'd gone.

They got on rather well after Luke had begun to relax, and she enjoyed their easy conversation, discovering over the tea and biscuits that they shared interests in books and music. And she was secretly pleased to note that he was obviously attracted to her, and found herself wondering how old he was and what his circumstances were.

It was well after midnight when he eventually left.

Mrs Wade, having noted how well they had been getting on with each other, warned her the next morning to be careful with whom she made friends, pointing out that the locals were well aware that she was a wealthy young lady. Asil laughed and said that she was quite capable of looking after her own interests, thank you very much, and set about quizzing her about the Lomax family, but she wasn't very forthcoming.

****

The following Sunday morning, Asil was woken by a gentle knock on her bedroom door. She looked sleepily at the time on the bedside radio, 9.15! There was another knock on the door, louder this time. Mrs Wade called: "Breakfast's ready Asil, are you awake?"

"Yes, Aunt Marjorie. Give me ten minutes and I'll be down. Is Mahari up and about?"

"Since seven o'clock!" she replied with a chuckle. Asil drew back the curtains and let the sunshine in. It was already warm so she put on a summer dress instead of her usual jeans and top and went downstairs where Mahari and Belynda were already sitting at the table waiting for her.

After breakfast Asil and Mahari walked into the village and bought newspapers. She briefed Mahari on the age of the pretty houses and cottages, some thatched, some washed in Suffolk pink; she explained how the village had prospered in the past from the wool trade, and related a little of the local history that she'd acquired. They entered the church with its 15th century tower that housed six bells, and sat in the cool for a few moments, enjoying the silence. Asil wondered what was going on in Mahari's mind.

When they returned to the house, Mrs Wade said that there'd been a phone call for Asil, a Mr Bowen, and that he would call again later. Asil didn't recognize the name. "Did he say what it was about?"

"No, but he sounded a bit annoyed that you weren't here, though. Asked where you were and what time you'd be back. I said you'd just gone out for a walk and didn't think you'd be very long."

"OK, thanks. We'll just have to wait then, won't we?"

Asil was puzzled and a little irritated. Apart from her colleagues at the charity office, not many people knew her telephone number. *Oh well*, she thought, *we'll soon find out*.

When the phone did ring later on, Asil picked it up. "Hello?"

"Is that Asil Daniels?" the voice asked.

"Speaking,"

"Ah, Charles Bowen. I'm an old friend of Doctor Bancroft. Ah, Asil, I'm..."

"It's Miss Daniels if you don't mind," said Asil rather abruptly; not liking the fact that he had been short with Mrs Wade.

"Oh, I'm *so* sorry, Miss Daniels." he said sarcastically. "Look, I'm afraid I couldn't make it to the funeral yesterday and I wondered if you would be going back to Wales for the reading of your uncle's will. I have some rather important information that I'm sure will interest you. You see I've heard so much about you and I would very much like to meet you. Now, if you would let me know when that will be? I'll give you a number where you can contact me of course. Would you do that for me?"

She resented his tone. He obviously imagined that she was a ten-year-old child.

"Mr Bowen, I've never heard Doctor Bancroft speak of you, and I don't think it's any of your business as to when or if I'm going to Wales. May I suggest that if you have any information for me, that you write to me here, I presume you have my address?"

"The matter that I have to discuss with you is confidential and personal." His tone had changed and was now quite threatening. "I would rather not commit it to paper. Let me just say that it would be unwise of you *not* to meet with me, Miss Daniels."

"Well, then I'm very sorry Mr Bowen. In that case I would prefer it if you wouldn't contact me again."

"Oh, you haven't heard the last of me, Miss Daniels."

The phone was hung up. Asil was left holding it in her hand, puzzled and a little shocked. "What an extremely rude man," she said.

"Is everything alright, dear?" asked Mrs Wade.

"Yes. Yes, nothing for you to worry about. It was that Bowen character, the one who phoned earlier. I hope he won't trouble us again. Though if he does ring, just hang up."

But she *was* worried, and Mrs Wade could see that she was. And why did he want to meet up after the reading of the will? She picked up the phone and dialled 1471. Number withheld, no surprise there then.

The day dawned overcast and slightly misty, dank and cold. Carole and Bill Daniels were up before six o'clock, already behind schedule. Carole slipped into Asils' bedroom and kissed the sleeping child on the forehead without waking her, before rushing downstairs as quietly as she could to join Bill in the car. She knew that the home help would be along soon to get Asil up and get her breakfast.

Bill started off down the steep hill at speed, the big BMW's tyres hissing on the wet road. Carole tensed as she sensed that the speed of the car was greater than usual. She looked apprehensively at Bill. He was gripping the wheel tightly and looking wide-eyed at the road ahead. She screamed as the car hurtled down the hill, obviously out of control, Bill frantically pumping the brake pedal. He desperately tried to wrestle the car round the bend but with tyres screaming it plunged through the undergrowth, over the high cliff, bouncing with a sickening crash on the rocks below and into the sea. The water boiled and bubbled as the mangled wreck sank to the deepest part of the ocean floor.

Asil was utterly distraught at the loss of her parents, She was taken in by her aunt Morag Flynn. A week after the funeral, Mrs Flowers, the Daniels' home help, called round to Morag's bungalow to see how Asil was coping. Morag made it quite plain that she was not welcome and told her that she must never come again and that Asil was now under her roof and that she would decide who she could see and who not. Mrs Flowers was horrified, but that wasn't all. "Wait there," said Morag, and disappeared back into the bungalow. She reappeared pulling a reluctant Patch, Asil's Springer spaniel, on a lead.

"Take this smelly dog with you and get rid of it to a dogs' home. I'm fed up with its hairs all over my furniture." She thrust the lead into Mrs Flowers' hand and slammed the door shut in her face.

Losing her beloved Patch was the last link with Asil's previously happy home. Life was about to get much worse for her from that day on.

A mood of dark depression suddenly descended over Asil. She had never felt lonely, being with the Wades, but she did feel very *alone.* She missed having a close friend.

Her best friend at school, Sophie Sinclair, worried about Asil. She knew what a sad life Asil had suffered and felt sorry for her. Eleven years old, she was a few months older than Asil and in a year above her at school. Walking home together one Friday afternoon Sophie said, "Do you like music, Asil?"

"My mum loved opera. I like it too, but I'm not allowed to listen to music at my aunt's."

"Don't you have a radio or CD player?"

"No."

"No telly in your bedroom?"

"There isn't even one in the house. Aunt Morag hates the TV."

"Look, I've got an old Sony Walkman at home that I don't use any more. Would you like it?"

"Yes, but I wouldn't have anything to play on it. Do you really not want it? I can't pay you for it – I'm not allowed pocket money."

"Don't worry, it's OK. I'll bring it to school on Monday. You don't have to tell your aunt about it if you don't want to."

Sophie gave it to her on that Monday. It had a tape already in it, and Sophie had put in new batteries. Asil was delighted with it, but she was also slightly concerned that she was being deceitful.

Not daring to let her Aunt Morag find out that she had something that would be a source of pleasure to her, she had to keep it hidden at home. She listened to it under the bedclothes at night with earphones. That sole tape was a compilation of rhythm and blues numbers by various artists; she almost wore it out, playing it over and over again, absorbing the changing tempos, identifying different instruments and making her body move to the beat. Over the next few months she swapped the tape for a classical recording of Mozart's *Clarinet Concerto* and fell in love with that, too.

After the arrest of her mad Aunt Morag, and once settled with Mrs Wade, she was able to buy her own CD player. With her aunt out of the way, Asil was allowed friends with whom she could expand her musical interests. And over the next few years she developed a liking for jazz, classical and a little opera. Her mother had liked opera, she remembered.

Although Belynda Wade was her age, they had very little in the way of common interests and didn't confide much in each other. Asil suspected that Belynda was a little jealous of her wealth and the fact that her mother was an employee and had virtually provided Asil with a home when she was orphaned. Belynda was into pop music, and clubbing in Ipswich. Asil's musical preferences were diametrically opposed. Belynda was into fashion and gossip magazines, *Hello Magazine* and TV soaps. Asil liked books, *Radio Three* and *the Guardian* and seldom watched TV. She longed to be able to discuss the books she'd read, the CDs she'd bought or heard, and would have loved to share going to classical or jazz concerts with someone.

Mrs Wade was aware that Asil was sometimes uncommunicative and morose and assumed that it was part of the grief she still bore for the loss of her parents all those years ago. She didn't really appreciate the depth of Asil's unhappiness. Only once in her life had Asil considered committing suicide. It was when she was about 12, a year or two after her second abduction. Her hormones were beginning to kick in and she felt that she had no one to confide in. Marjorie Wade was kind and motherly but was occupied with bringing up her own daughter.

Asil had wondered if her life would forever hold the threat of being harried and pursued. She didn't want to live in perpetual fear. That's when she had felt suicidal.

Looking back on it now, she marvelled at her own determination to pull herself out of it.

If she could sum up how she had felt then, the lines of an old Mississippi blues would have done it perfectly.

I'm gonna lay, lay my head
On some old railroad iron,
And let that two-nineteen
Pacify my mind.

Up in her room she decided to try and cheer herself up, so she put on an Ella Fitzgerald CD and chose *On the Sunny Side of the Street*. She hummed along to it, it never failed to lift her spirits. When she came to the line *'just direct your feet to the sunny side of the street'* she said aloud 'I'm going to direct *my* feet straight to the pub tonight!'

LUKE

That evening she did decide to go to the local pub, in the hope that Luke would be there.

She had noticed him on a few occasions over the last few weeks since he had helped her change the tyre on her car. They had exchanged smiles when passing in the street or meeting in the local shop and had been pleased to note that he seemed interested in her. She had already asked Mrs Wade if she knew much about him. Mrs Wade knew that he lived with his mother and had some sort of engineering business that he ran from home. Belynda was much more forthcoming because she also thought him attractive and teased Asil about her interest in him.

She changed into jeans and a top and walked the few hundred yards to The Swan. She peered through the window of the bar and her heart rate increased when she saw Luke sitting there by himself, reading a book of some sort. She wouldn't have wanted to go in alone if he hadn't been there, especially on a Sunday evening. Was he waiting for someone? Would he be pleased to see her? She hesitated, then plucked up courage, took a deep breath and walked boldly in. She was delighted and relieved when Luke looked up and spotted her immediately. He smiled, stood up and walked over to greet her.

"Hello Asil, what a lovely surprise! Can I get you something? I hope it's me you've come to see?"

"Now why would you think that, Luke Lomax?" she laughed. "OK, just a J2O then."

He picked up her glass and led her to his table at the back of the bar. He closed his book and put it on the seat beside him.

"Don't let me stop you from catching up on your reading, Luke."

"No, it's fine, it's a tricky job I've got to tackle tomorrow so I thought I'd read up a bit about the car I'm working on over a pint. I can finish this later. You're much more important! So what's new, Asil?"

She hesitated before answering.

"I don't want to put a damper on your evening, but, well, to tell you the truth Luke, I'm a bit worried about a phone call I had earlier today." She told him how the call had gone.

He looked concerned and said: "And you've never heard of this man?"

"No, and I'm sure Uncle Gordon would have mentioned him had he been a friend. I have this horrible fear…"

"Who's this 'Uncle Gordon'?" Luke interrupted.

"He died recently. I've not long come back from the funeral in Wales. As I said, I have this horrible fear that this is something to do with money." Luke frowned and looked down at his glass, not knowing if he should comment.

"Luke, if I tell you my circumstances, will you promise not to tell a soul? There aren't many people I can trust here. But I feel I can trust you and I need someone who's not connected with me to give me a little help."

Luke put his hand on hers, sensing her anguish.

"Of course, you know I'd love to be of help if I can."

Asil told him the whole story. The death of her parents, her time spent with her insane aunt Morag, her abduction and threatened torture; and two years later, her kidnapping. She told him how her father had had a special silver box made in Japan to contain the coded location of the treasure that's now her inheritance. How the two Romanian agents had been caught and deported after their involvement in her abduction.

Luke had lots of questions all the way through, all of which Asil answered truthfully, not wishing to hide anything from him.

They had quite forgotten the time until Asil's mobile phone rang. It was Mrs Wade.

"Asil, where *are* you? I'm worried about you, its gone ten o'clock! You said you'd only be gone a—"

"It's OK Auntie, I'm at The Swan. With Mr Lomax. Sorry, didn't realise it was so late. I'll be home in about half an hour, OK?"

"Yes of course Asil, sorry to—"

"That's alright, Auntie, see you soon, eh?"

Luke smiled. "Checking up on you, is she?"

"It's my fault, I told her I'd only be out for an hour. I'll tell her that it was entirely your fault, Luke! Now I think I should be going. Walk me home?"

"If I get a goodnight kiss as a reward?"

"We'll see about that!" she laughed. They finished their drinks, Luke picked up his manual and they left. Asil linked her arm through his as they walked slowly back to Asil's house, enjoying the mild evening air. The sky was crystal clear and the stars shone brightly, the moon casting faint shadows through the trees. Their feet scrunched on the gravel as they walked up the drive. When they got to her door Luke turned to face her and took hold of both her hands and looked at her earnestly. He said: "I don't like the sound of this Bowen chap, Asil. You need to be very careful. When there's lots of money involved people can get very nasty. Promise me you'll call me if you need any help?"

"I intend to, Luke, and thanks for putting up with me all evening."

She leaned forward and kissed him quickly on the cheek, turned and went in before he could react. He stood still for a few moments touching his cheek where she'd kissed him, smiled broadly and turned to walk home with an extra spring in his step.

THE WILL

It was a few days later that Asil received notification from the solicitors, Lloyd, Lloyd and Carragher, requesting her and Mahari's presence for the reading of the will on Thursday the 24th June at 10am, a week hence. It was signed W G Lloyd. Asil remembered Mr. Lloyd Senior who had dealt with her father's will, but she had never met the son. She presumed that his father had retired.

Asil and Luke met that evening in The Swan. Asil showed Luke the solicitors' letter.

"How will you get there? Drive? Will you stay over in Wales? How long—?"

She held up her hand to stop him. "Whoa, Luke, one question at a time! I haven't really thought it through yet. I'll have to take Mahari, of course. Yes, I'll have to stay for maybe two or three days. I'll drive, I think. It'll be handy having the car there."

"What about Mrs Wade and Belynda, won't they want to come?"

"Yes they will. But no, I don't think that would be a good idea. Better that they stay here and look after the house."

"Where will you stay, at the doctor's house?"

"Oh no! It wouldn't be good for Mahari. Anyway, it'll be cold and damp. I'll book us in to the Llety Bodfor hotel in Aberdovey; it's only a few miles down the road. I don't want to stay in Towyn, it's got too many bad memories for me." In fact the thought of going back to Wales at all depressed and frightened her. To drive past the places where she had been kept prisoner with the threat of torture made her skin crawl. She shuddered involuntarily.

Luke remained silent for a moment. He leaned over the table and took her hand.

"I'm coming with you, Asil. You're not driving down on your own. In fact you're not driving at all. I'll take you both."

Asil withdrew her hand quickly from his.

"No! Just a minute Luke, that's out of the question. That's crazy, you've got your business to see to, your mother—"

"I won't take no for an answer, Asil. And I haven't forgotten about the mysterious Mr Bowen. It's the least I can do. Anyway, you'll be thinking of the will and you won't be concentrating on the road."

Asil mulled it over, shaking her head. She took a sip of her drink and drummed her fingers on the table.

"Look Luke, that really is sweet of you. I really would appreciate your company, though. But if I agree, you *must* let me pay for your stay at the hotel and for the fuel for the journey *and* your hourly rate per day, or whatever you charge for your work. Otherwise it's no go, and I mean it."

Luke hesitated, shook his head in submission, smiled and said:

"You're a hard woman, Asil Daniels. Now how could I refuse?" He laughed and took hold of both her hands and squeezed them tightly. He noticed a tear forming in Asil's eyes in spite of her smile.

When she went to bed that night she cried. They weren't tears of grief, just the joy of knowing that she had a friend whom she was beginning to love and who was being so kind to her.

Asil had been seeing a lot of Luke during the last couple weeks. She'd found out that he was 24 years old, earned his living as a freelance engineer, and had his own well-equipped workshop where he specialized in making replacement parts for veteran and vintage cars and motorcycles. He still lived with his mother, his father having passed away a couple of years previously. And he didn't appear to be in any sort of relationship, she was pleased to note.

At school he'd been a great disappointment to his tutors. An obviously intelligent boy, his inability to concentrate unfortunately produced poor results in exams. He had always been more interested in hands-on activities and shone at science or working with metal and wood. When he left school, his parents tried to guide him into further education with a view to getting an office job, seeing that he had not qualified for a place at university. They were quite horrified when he took a job in a large garage in Ipswich as a trainee technician. However, he quickly proved his worth there and was very well thought of. He developed an interest in classic motorcycles, found a 1938 Velocette KTT on the internet, bought it, stripped it down and restored it completely to concourse condition. He made a huge profit when he sold it. His next project, when he was 17, was to do the same with a 1957 MGA open sports car, purchased with the money he made by selling the Velocette. His restoration work involved sourcing parts through various classic car magazines and the internet. It made him realize that there were lots of people out there with plenty of money to lavish on their cherished old cars and motorcycles and that spares were difficult to find. So with the money made from the MGA project, he furnished his workshop, or rather the converted double garage next to the house, with lathes, milling machines, drill stands, bench grinders etc. and advertised his expertise in producing parts to pattern, in classic car and motorcycle magazines and on the internet. It took time for the business to take off and it didn't earn him a great deal of money even now, but it was enough to live on, and growing all the time. He had found his niche in life and was quite happy with his lot.

He felt quite excited about being close to Asil for two or three days down in Wales.

****

Luke's VW Passat estate pulled into the forecourt of the Llety Bodfor hotel. It had taken five hours to drive from Suffolk to Aberdovey with just one short stop. Luke was a good driver, fast but safe, and Asil had been able to relax on the way. In fact she had nodded off twice. Mahari had slept most of the way, as he usually did when a passenger. It was seven in the evening and they were all tired and hungry. Luke got one of the cases, Mahari clutched his overnight bag and Asil took the other case out of the car and they made for reception. After booking in to their separate rooms they agreed to meet in the restaurant at eight. Asil showered and changed, then rang Mrs Wade to let her know that they had arrived safely.

Although they enjoyed a good meal and a bottle of wine, conversation was limited after such a tiring drive, and Asil was preoccupied with what the next day might bring. She was glad when the meal was over and she could get to bed. They were back in their rooms by 10.30. Asil took a long time to get to sleep. She was apprehensive over the forthcoming reading of the will because it posed many questions, particularly for Mahari. And there was the spectre of Mr Bowen always lurking in the background. She hoped that he would not trouble Mrs Wade and Belynda while she was away.

The next morning dawned overcast and humid. Asil couldn't help feeling that the weather was an omen for what was going to be revealed in the will. She had developed a thumping headache. Maybe it was the red wine she'd consumed with the meal the previous evening or it could have been the weather. She showered and dressed soberly for the visit to the solicitors. She joined Luke and Mahari for breakfast. Luke ordered kippers and tucked in heartily. Mahari had been down to breakfast early and had already polished off a full English and was finishing off his pot of tea. Asil couldn't stand the smell of kippers this early in the day and ordered scrambled eggs on toast but she was struggling to eat much of it. Luke looked concerned and asked her if she was feeling all right.

"No I'm not! It's smelling those kippers of yours at this time of the morning!" she snapped. Luke looked hurt and shook his head and threw a glance at Mahari. Mahari frowned, got up from the table and went back up to his room. Asil took this as a rebuke, and picked irritably again at her scrambled eggs, then pushed her half full plate away.

"Sorry, Asil, I didn't know you didn't like the smell of kippers. My mother can't stand the smell either, that's why I tend to have them for breakfast whenever I have the chance to eat out."

Asil immediately regretted being cross with him. She put her hand on top of his and squeezed it, forcing a smile while holding back a tear.

"I'm sorry, Luke. I've managed to upset Mahari as well. I woke up in a black mood this morning. I didn't get much sleep during the night and I'm worried about the will. And this humid weather doesn't help. It always gives me a bad head. Forgive me?"

"Of course. Look, try to think positively, Asil. From what you've told me, your uncle Gordon thought the world of you, so why would he not treat you well in his will?"

"It's not *me* I'm worried about, Luke! It's Mahari," she snapped. "Uncle Gordon was the only semblance of a family he's had since he left home when he was only eight or nine years old. He's obviously worried about the will, too. What *will* become of him?"

"Don't worry! Knowing you as I do, I know you'll find a way of looking after his interests whatever happens. Won't you?"

"Well, yes, I suppose I will, Luke." She had another go at eating her breakfast, fiddled with the remainder of her scrambled eggs again and pushed the plate away irritably for a second time.

"Now for goodness sake call the waitress and ask her to get rid of what's left of those kippers!" Asil laughed and began to feel better. They enjoyed a pot of tea and toast and marmalade before going back up to their rooms. Asil knocked at Mahari's door and waited for him to open it. She went in and gave him a hug. "I know you're worried about today, Mahari. It'll soon be over and I'm sure that Uncle Gordon will have looked after your interests. And I've apologised to Luke for the way I spoke to him. Feel better now?" He smiled, nodded approval of her apology and returned her hug.

They drove through an overcast, misty morning to Lloyd, Lloyd and Carragher's offices in Towyn, arriving 15 minutes before their appointment. The Victorian offices were unwelcoming, largely unchanged since the original Mr Lloyd had taken them on in the late 1950s. Oak furniture, oak panelled walls and polished wooden flooring that creaked, gave the whole place an air of melancholy.

An elderly secretary offered them coffee, which they declined.

Mr Lloyd junior came out and invited Asil and Mahari into his office. Luke squeezed Asil's hand, patted Mahari on the back and whispered, "Good luck!" He was left to wait uncomfortably in the secretary's office.

They sat on comfortable red leather chairs at a large oblong table. Mr Lloyd was tall and thin, just like his father, Asil remembered. He made great play of shuffling papers and clearing his throat several times before looking up and smiling nervously at them each in turn. Asil noticed that he had dandruff on his suit collar and the elbows of his jacket were shiny with wear.

"Well, Miss Daniels, Mr Artaxis. This is the last testament of Gordon Harvey Bancroft. I will read it to you as you are both mentioned here. To my knowledge, Doctor Bancroft had no other living relations.

I quote: 'To my good friend Reverend Anthony O'Malley I bequeath the sum of one thousand pounds to be used for the benefit of his church, and a briefcase that I have deposited with Mr W G Lloyd of Lloyd, Lloyd and Carragher, the contents of which must remain secret and must only be discussed with Miss Asil Daniels on her 21st birthday, or before in any circumstances deemed exceptional. I also wish for Reverend Anthony to arrange my funeral at his church. (This has already been taken care of, of course), to Mrs Marjorie Wade I also bequeath the sum of one thousand pounds for her goodness of heart in taking in and looking after Miss Daniels. Also a monthly sum of £800 until Asil Daniels reaches her 21st birthday.

"To my faithful friend Mahari Artaxis I leave my house and all its contents.

"To Asil Daniels I leave all my books and whatever finances remain after all the other matters referred to in this will have been fulfilled.'

"That concludes the reading of this will. If either of you have any questions I will be glad to help."

He looked from one to the other over the top of his spectacles for their reaction, frowning, as if he were expecting some awkward questions.

"That's wonderful, Mahari, isn't?" said Asil squeezing his hand and smiling at him. Mahari looked stunned, shook his head and shrugged. She knew that he was grieving too much to care about the house or the details of the will at this moment. Asil thanked Mr Lloyd and said that at the moment there was nothing more to say.

Lloyd smiled his relief, coughed nervously, pushed his spectacles further up onto the bridge of his nose, shuffled the papers again and stood up.

"You'll let me know when the finances have been settled, Mr Lloyd. I'll send my bank details to you at the appropriate time so that you can arrange the transfer of whatever is due to me. And I'll tell Mrs Wade that she can expect a letter from you, she'll be delighted to know that Uncle Gordon hadn't forgotten her. You have my phone number, Mr Lloyd?"

He looked through his papers and said: "Ah, yes, I have it here."

She shook his hand and thanked him for his efforts. She put her arm around Mahari's shoulder and led him out to the car with Luke following close behind.

Luke was anxious to hear the outcome but Asil put her finger to her lips. She opened the rear door of the car, settled Mahari in then closed it. Before getting into the car, she turned to Luke.

She whispered, "Uncle Gordon has left him the house, I don't think he wants to go back there though. Let's go back to the hotel and we'll try and sort him out."

"There you are then. I told you you'd no need to worry. Feel better now?"

"Yes I do, Luke, thanks. But I'm still concerned about Mahari's state of mind." She kissed Luke on the cheek before they got into the car.

They went up to Asil's room where they ordered coffee and croissants to be delivered. Asil looked at Mahari and said, "You can stay with us at home in Suffolk, Mahari, for as long as you like. That's if you want to. I know that there's nothing left for you here in Towyn. If you want, you can sell the house and move down to Monks Eleigh. But do take your time. You don't need to make any quick decision. Sort out at home what you want to bring down to us and I'll arrange transport for it. We can put your furniture and stuff, and whatever else you want to keep, in storage until you've made up your mind what you want to do."

Mahari smiled and nodded approval. Just then there was a knock at the door and the coffee and croissants arrived.

Asil began to relate details of the will but Luke stopped her.

“Look Asil, I shouldn’t be listening to your personal affairs. You don’t have to tell me everything.”

Asil looked hurt.

“Luke, I’m hoping I can rely on you to help me through what may be difficult times ahead for me. I can, can’t I?”

“Yes, of course you can.”

“Then keep quiet while I tell you the rest of the details please,” she said, smiling at his discomfort.

Afterwards, Luke suggested that they go to the house so that Mahari could mark up all the items that he’d want to send down to Suffolk, and then to pack whatever else he might need to bring with him when they returned. Asil agreed and after a light lunch in the hotel they drove back to Towyn. Luke stopped at WH Smiths and bought some post-it notes, tie-on labels, a marker pen and cellotape for Mahari to mark up the items in the house.

BREAK-IN

The Bancroft house was a converted underground RSG, (Regional Seat of Government,) which had been constructed during the cold war as a secure base for use by the authorities in case of a nuclear attack. The doctor had purchased it from the MoD and converted it into living accommodation, installing modern central heating and air conditioning.

Having been empty for three weeks, it smelt damp as they entered through the steel door. Mahari switched on the lights. Asil gasped at the sight that confronted them. The place had been ransacked. As they went from room to room, draws had been emptied, upholstery ripped from chairs and settees, the beds stripped and mattresses slit open.

On closer inspection, nothing of value appeared to have been taken. It seemed that it was documents that they had been searching for. Asil felt nauseated. She knew instinctively that it was something to do with her inheritance. It was no coincidence that this had happened between Doctor Bancroft's funeral and the will being read.

"I'll ring the police," Luke said as he picked up the phone. But it was dead. He reached for his mobile but Asil caught hold of his arm and stopped him.

"No. Not yet. I'd rather contact John Nolloth, an old friend of mine. He's a retired Chief Inspector and I know that he's still working as a private investigator, he told me so at the funeral. I rang him before we left to tell him that we'd be here for a couple of days. I'm sure this is something to do with that Bowen character and probably the Romanian connection. Plus he has some knowledge of the way they operate."

"I really think you should call the police, Asil it's—"

"*No* Luke. Leave it to me."

"OK, sorry…but what does Mahari think, it's his house after all?"

Asil looked at Mahari who had been listening attentively.

"Well, Mahari? John Nolloth? Yes or no."

Mahari, still in an apparent dazed state from the reading of the will, nodded yes. He looked at Luke and shrugged an apology.

"Right, let's leave this mess as it is and go back to the hotel. I'll ring John from there. Pack whatever clothes you need for the next couple of weeks, Mahari. You can sort out marking up your things later on."

Luke was seeing a side of Asil that he hadn't seen before, a steely determination and an air of authority forged by her past unpleasant experiences. It took him by surprise. *Not a woman to be messed with*, he thought.

When they arrived back at the hotel, Asil left a message on Nolloth's phone and asked him to ring back on her mobile number. She didn't have to wait long.

"Asil, good to hear from you. Where are you?"

"We're staying at the Llety Bodfor. I need your help John, I wondered if you could come over."

Asil explained the reason for her call. Nolloth said he would meet her at the hotel in about an hour. He already knew, of course, that today was the day for Asil's appointment with the solicitor's and guessed that there might be a problem with the will. After he put the phone down he went to his filing cabinet and took out the file on the Daniels case. He studied it carefully, remembering the details quite clearly. He sighed, concerned for Asil who had endured so much and with such fortitude. His instincts told him that she was entering a very dangerous time if indeed the Romanians were involved once again. He put the file away and closed the drawer; getting up painfully from his chair and rubbing his legs; 40 years of police work had been hard on his knees. He hoped that there were not going to be too many stairs at the hotel.

He arrived at the hotel at six o'clock. He waited for them in the foyer. He greeted Asil and Mahari warmly when they came down and was introduced to Luke. They went into the lounge and sat down at a table.

"Now, what can I do to help?"

Tears welled up in Asil's eyes. The thought that she was responsible for bringing this trauma to bear on Mahari was suddenly overwhelming. She held her face in her hands and began to sob silently. Luke moved to her chair and held her.

"She's had quite a shock today, with the doctor's house being broken into and ransacked. She wouldn't let me call the police."

Asil composed herself, wiped her eyes with her handkerchief and waved Luke away.

"Whoever it was, they must have been looking for papers, John. Nothing else looked as if it was missing, but there were papers strewn all over the place."

She told him about the call from the man Bowen back in Suffolk. She told him that Doctor Bancroft had left the house to Mahari in the will.

"Right Asil. I don't want you to worry. Stay here and I'll take Mahari back to the house and have a good look around. In the meantime, try and relax."

"Relax? No, I'd rather come with you—"

"No, Asil. Luke will keep you company, won't you Luke?"

Luke nodded.

"I take it Luke's your boyfriend, Asil?" This was said with a sparkle in his eye and a smile.

Asil laughed and blushed. "Just a good friend, John," she said.

He winked at Luke and said, "Oh well. Come on, Mahari, let's go."

He left straight away with a bewildered Mahari.

"Doesn't waste much time, does he?" said Luke.

Asil stood up and said, "Oh Luke, I feel so much better now that he's on the case. Come and give me a hug, will you?"

"As a good friend?" Luke said with a smile. He was only too happy to oblige. It was a long embrace.

Nolloth and Mahari eventually arrived back at the hotel at nine o'clock and made their way up to Asil's room. Almost before they had got through the door, Asil asked, "Well, John? What've you found out?" Not really knowing if she wanted to hear the answer.

"I'm hungry, that's what I've found out Asil. And I reckon Mahari is too. I take it I'm on expenses? So shall we all get dinner here and I'll be happy to put you in the picture as soon as we've eaten?"

Asil laughed and said, "It's gone nine, John! Luke and I have already eaten, but we'll keep you company and share a bottle of wine with you, if you like."

Nolloth smiled and said, "Wine? It's a good pint of real ale I need!"

"Come on then," said Asil and led the way down to the restaurant.

After Nolloth and Mahari had finished their meals they took coffee in the lounge. At last Nolloth began to relate his findings.

"Firstly, they, for there were two of them, had knowledge of the hidden passageway from the woods close to the rear of your aunt Morag's old bungalow. They gained entry through the rear door to the house that's situated in the tunnel. I'm sure there were at least two people involved. Apparently the present occupants of your aunt's bungalow had seen a dark blue Audi saloon parked just inside the wood out of sight of the road when they took their dog for a walk. It was parked in such a way that they thought it might have been stolen and abandoned, so they took the number just in case it'd been dumped there. That's all we've got to go on at the moment. It wouldn't surprise me if this man Bowen were involved somehow. If they didn't find what they were looking for, I'll bet that they'll try to contact you again. We can't know what it is they want of course, but it seems likely that it's to do with part of the goods that your father bought back from Romania. I think we'll just have to sit tight for now and see if anything develops. You'll be looking after Asil I take it, Luke?"

"I certainly will, Mr Nolloth."

"Call me John, Luke."

"Do you think we should stay on here or go back to Suffolk?" asked Asil.

"No, don't stay here. Go home. Bowen contacted you there so I see no point in staying and I know how expensive the stay is for the three of you. I'll arrange for the back door at the house to be secured and get the place tidied up. If that's OK, Mahari?"

Mahari agreed and expressed his gratitude by shaking Nolloth's hand warmly.

"Right, I've got a bit more digging to do. I'll try and find out whether strangers with a dark blue Audi have been staying overnight at the local hostelries for a start. Don't expect to hear from me for a couple of days, Asil. And don't phone me from Monks Eleigh. I wouldn't chance the fact that they may have your phone tapped at home. Mobile only if it's urgent, OK?"

"Right, John. We'll leave in the morning then, shall we boys?" Luke and Mahari nodded their agreement. Nolloth thanked Asil for the meal and Asil hugged him warmly. He shook Luke's hand and gave Mahari a friendly punch on the shoulder before leaving.

Asil said, "I think that's quite enough for today you guys. It's nearly midnight. Have you got all you need for tomorrow, Mahari?"

He nodded yes, kissed Asil goodnight and hugged her before leaving for his room. After a few minutes Asil and Luke went upstairs and stopped outside Asil's room. Luke hesitated at the door, turned to Asil and said, "And do I get a *proper* goodnight kiss this time?"

"I think you deserve it," she said. She moved towards him and put her arms around him, resting her cheek on his shoulder. He embraced her tightly, lifted her chin and kissed her gently on the mouth. She pulled away and smiled.

"Thanks for being here, Luke. It means a lot to me. Now go to bed before I get too emotional!"

She pushed him away, opened her door and closed it behind her. She leaned her back against it, folded her arms, shut her eyes and smiled to herself. She had been on the brink of inviting him in but had thought better of it. She was getting much too fond of Mr Lomax.

CAMPEANU

Ion Campeanu had been raised in the time when Nicolae Ceausescu was ruling the country, before the 1989 revolution. He had been brought up in an orphanage, mistreated and abused, and quickly learned that by pleasing the authorities his life improved. Even from an early age he had no qualms about spying on his neighbours and reporting any hint of anti-government activities to the secret police. He was recruited into the *Securitate* at 17 years of age and helped the brutal regime suppress any anti-government feeling, never shirking from employing any form of violence that would produce a confession. He enjoyed inflicting pain.

After the revolution he managed to avoid reprisals, kept a low profile for a couple of years and then once again found favour in the new intelligence service, where his uncompromising and ruthless nature were highly valued.

Ion Campeanu left his Mercedes in the car park of the hotel in Hintlesham and hurried into the foyer.

He had booked a room earlier. He picked up the key and asked the receptionist if he could speak to Charles Bowen. She dialled the room number and Bowen answered immediately. The receptionist passed the phone to Campeanu.

"Ion here. Meet me in the bar in 15 minutes, will you?"

Campeanu ordered a whisky and soda and took it to a seat by the window. Bowen joined him ten minutes later, greeting him with a nervous smile.

"Well?" Campeanu said curtly.

"Nothing. No documents of any sort that relate to what we want, let alone anything of use."

"Were you seen?"

"No, I don't think so. I waited until they went to visit the solicitors. I parked the car in the woods and used the hidden passage that leads to the rear door of the house. It wasn't difficult to break in. We went through every room and every nook and cranny. Bancroft must have deposited the items with either the girl Daniels or perhaps the solicitor, or maybe even in a bank's secure vault."

"We? You mean you were not alone?"

"I needed help, Ion. I used a local man, Jake Bull, who I knew had a grudge against the Daniels and he'd been to Bancroft's house before. He went to prison for his part in the abduction of the Daniels girl ten years ago. He knew about the hidden tunnel. I couldn't have got in through the front entrance without being seen."

Detecting Campeanu's anger, Bowen fiddled nervously with his glass, swilling it round so that the ice cubes rattled inside. Campeanu shook his head disbelievingly, shut his eyes and cupped his chin in his hands.

Bowen put the glass down on the table and began excavating his left ear with his index finger.

Campeanu looked up and fixed him with a cold stare.

"You will vouch for the fact that this man Bull will not talk?"

"Of course not, he—"

"You fool, Bowen. Presumably you paid him?"

"Well, yes. I *had* to. He could be useful if we need a bit of muscle later. He's not squeamish about roughing people up. I suggest that we work on this Mahari character in order to get to the Daniels girl. He'll probably be on his own at the house when she returns home, so it shouldn't be too difficult."

Bowen's naivety caused a wry smile to cross Campeanu's face.

"Hmm. So you think that's a possibility, do you? But I think it's too soon for those sorts of tactics. We need something a bit more subtle than beating people up, Bowen. We've got away with getting rid of Bancroft. Thank God I used a substance that I was certain the pathologist wouldn't be able to detect. Let's see what develops over the next few days first. Keep an eye on Daniels' house and let me know as soon as she returns. Get on to that as soon as possible."

"Are you staying here now?" asked Bowen.

"I was going to, for a couple of days, but now for tonight only. I've decided to leave very early in the morning, before breakfast. I now have something urgent to attend to, thanks to you, Bowen. I'll look forward to hearing something positive from you in the next couple of days. I'll leave you to enjoy the rest of your evening."

Campeanu stood up, said goodnight, and went up to his room. He sat down, picked up the phone and dialled a number in Romania.

The conversation had left Bowen apprehensive. He knew that Campeanu was inwardly furious about him using Jake Bull. *How could he have expected me to do the job on my own?* he thought. He pondered on the fact that Campeanu was going to leave in the morning, and that he had said curiously 'thanks to you'. What did he mean? Bowen drained his glass and sullenly ordered another from the barman. He began to wish that he'd never got involved with this strange and frightening man.

****

The journey back to Monks Eleigh was boringly long as usual. Mahari was morose, sitting in the back seat and staring out of the window, too much going through his mind to fall asleep as he usually did on long car journeys. Asil didn't feel like making conversation, too many thoughts were rattling around in her head. What would they find when they arrived home? Another break-in? Who was this Bowen character and was it he who had burgled Mahari's house? What exactly were they looking for? She sighed loudly, irritated at her train of thought. She opened the glove compartment and took out half a dozen CDs. She sorted through them; her eyes lit up as she remembered that Luke was also a jazz fan. Lester Young, Billie Holliday, John Coltrane, Dinah Washington, Count Basie.

"Can I play one of these please, Luke?"

"Depends which one," he said, teasing. She smiled and selected a Miles Davis CD and set it playing.

"Good choice Asil. *A Kind of Blue*? One of his best."

She closed her eyes and let the music wash over her. Luke beat out a rhythm on the steering wheel to accompany the strains of *Round Midnight*. Mahari tapped Asil on the shoulder and when she turned round he smiled broadly and put his fingers in his ears. She laughed, pleased that he was getting over the shock of the reading of the will, and turned the volume up another notch.

Luke pulled into a motorway service area where they sat down to a snack in the crowded, noisy and not very clean restaurant. Luke filled the car with fuel before they left and both Mahari and Asil finally drifted off to sleep for the rest of the journey.

They arrived back in Monks Eleigh just after two thirty. Mrs Wade was out shopping with Belynda, no doubt stocking up with food for their return. Asil asked Luke to stay and have something to eat, then went straight upstairs to her room and changed. Her mobile rang just as she rejoined Luke and Mahari. It was John Nolloth.

"Asil, I've traced the number of the Audi left in the wood near Morag's old bungalow. It's a hire car and was rented from a firm in Ipswich to a Charles Bowen two weeks ago. He gave his address as a flat in Oakley Gardens in Chelsea. Quite an expensive area I believe. The fact that he hired the car locally may mean that someone else drove him up from London. That may explain why there were two people involved in the burglary here. Anyway, I'll try and find out something about the man, but I thought I'd let you know that things are on the move. Anything to report your end?"

"No, we've only just got home, but all seems OK. That's great news, John. Anything you want me to do?"

"No, just keep your eyes and ears open. Maybe Luke could trawl around the area in search of the Audi. Just make sure the house is secure before you go to bed. I'll contact you again tomorrow if there's anything to report."

"Thanks John, you're a star. Bye."

She gave the piece of paper with the number of the Audi to Luke.

"John thinks it may be worth looking round the area for that car. Can you do that for me, Luke?"

"Sure. After that meal you promised me, though!"

Mrs Wade and Belynda arrived carrying bags of shopping. She apologized for not being there to greet them.

Asil said, "I was just going to get Luke something to eat."

"Oh no you don't, my girl! You've driven all that way my dears and no one here to welcome you, I'm so sorry. You must be starving, how about I do us some bacon baguettes all round?"

"Brilliant Aunt Marjorie, I'll give you a hand."

"No you won't Asil, you keep this young man company. Belynda will make a pot of tea, won't you dear?"

Belynda frowned and threw a glance at Asil but said in a subdued voice, "OK mum."

Asil smiled at Luke and when mother and daughter had disappeared into the kitchen, she said, "Dear Marjorie, treats me like a child still, but she's got a heart of gold."

"Belynda didn't look too pleased," Luke whispered.

"She would rather have stayed to talk to you, Luke. I think she's got a crush on you!" she said mischievously. Luke shook his head and smiled.

They tucked into the bacon baguettes and cups of tea and finished with a piece of Mrs Wade's lemon drizzle cake. After they'd eaten, Luke left for home to check his emails and post. He had one or two small jobs to complete quite urgently, so he told Asil that he'd ring her when he'd finished, probably about noon the next day.

Asil had so much going through her mind that her head ached. Poor Mahari. He had lost the man who had been like a father to him, and he had no one else. While he had good friends in Asil and the Wades, they were not the same as family. His situation was made worse by not being able to adequately express his feelings. Asil went to his room and knocked at the door. Mahari opened it and Asil went in and sat down on the bed.

"Look Mahari, I'm so sorry that I've brought all this trouble on you. It's all because of the treasure and I wish to God that I'd never seen it. But there's nothing I can do about what's happened in the past except try and make it up to you. You don't want to go back to Towyn, do you?"

He shook his head vigorously.

"Then you must stay here and we'll find you a place of your own close by. If you really don't want the Bancroft house we can put it on the market, it should fetch more than enough to fix you up with a really nice place here and have plenty to spare. You'll never want for anything as long as I'm alive."

He nodded approval, took both of Asil's hands and squeezed them tightly.

"Think about it my lovely man, we'll talk about it later."

****

The next day John Nolloth rang again.

"Asil, I've got some more information on our mysterious Mr Bowen. Apparently he used to work at the Foreign Office, but was dismissed for what was described as 'unprofessional conduct' about two years ago. Since then he's been working as a consultant for a company called Solvers. They specialize in providing information to British firms that wish to trade in countries in the Baltic. It operates from a rented office in Streatham, and I suspect that it's a front for something more sinister. Doesn't appear to be anyone there to answer the phone though, just an answering machine. I'm having the premises watched by a contact I have in London but nobody's been in or out so far. However, it seems to point to a connection with Romania and your inheritance."

"Much as we feared then John. Luke's going to have a look round the village today to see if the Audi is parked anywhere. There's not much more I can do, is there?"

"Just be vigilant Asil. I can't see what they would gain by harming you or Mahari. It's going to be a cat and mouse game I'm afraid. We'll just have to wait and see what his or their next move is."

"OK, we'll carry on a normal life until things change, eh? Talk to you soon. And thanks again, John."

"Give my regards to your boyfriend, Asil."

"I'm glad that you can't see me blush, John!" she chuckled. "Bye for now."

The next morning Luke arrived to report that he hadn't managed to locate the Audi.

"I thought that Bowen might be staying at a hotel nearby. There aren't many to choose from around here. Maybe I'll go round the hotel car parks late this evening, it's more likely to be parked at that time. What do you think?"

"Fine by me. Would you like some company?"

"No Asil, it'll be better on my own, but thanks for the offer."

"Going off me then, are you?" she teased.

"That'll never happen, Asil," he said smiling. "But if you like I can take you out to lunch today, how about it?"

"Great! Where are you going to take me then? Somewhere nice I hope?"

"Hintlesham Hall? Posh enough for you?"

"Wow, super! I'll have to change though, can't go in jeans and trainers, can I?"

"Be ready in 15 minutes and I'll pick you up."

"Make it half an hour Luke, you know how long it takes us girls to get ready! And I'll pick *you* up, you can have a drink then, can't you?"

"Great, thanks. See you in half an hour then."

Asil took her time preparing herself for her lunch date. She put on her favourite skirt and a low-cut top, her highest heels, tied her hair up into a ponytail and dabbed on her most expensive perfume and applied her make-up carefully. She looked at herself in her full-length mirror and was pleased at what she saw.

ARBELOV

Asil was pleased that she'd suggested taking her car. It meant that Luke could enjoy a drink with his lunch; she knew that he liked his real ale. She picked him up at his house, knocking on the door to find that he was waiting for her and opened it immediately.

"Wow, Asil, you look fantastic! It's only lunch, you know, but I'm not complaining!"

It didn't take long to drive the few miles to Hintlesham. The hall was an impressive sight, a 16th century Elizabethan manor house set in 175 acres of rolling countryside and approached down a long tree-lined drive.

Once settled in the restaurant, Luke ordered a pint of Old Speckled Hen and Asil had a glass of Pinot Grigio. Luke ordered coronation chicken and Asil decided on scampi. They finished with a crème brulee each. Coffee in the lounge afterwards rounded off the lunch nicely; Luke had a brandy to go with his coffee, enjoying the rare luxury of not having to drive. They sat and chatted about all their likes and dislikes and Asil became increasingly aware of how much they enjoyed in common. They had been discussing a forthcoming concert at the Regent Theatre in Ipswich being given by the Royal Philharmonic. Asil particularly liked the programme of 20th century music; Rachmaninov, Samuel Barber and Aaron Copland.

A man sitting in a chair with its back close to Asil's rose and walked round the table, turning to face her. He was tall, slim, elegantly dressed in a light grey suit, dark blue shirt and dark tie. Asil assessed him as middle aged, quite handsome, with hair slightly greying at the temples, immaculately manicured.

"I am so sorry to appear rude but I couldn't help overhearing your conversation. It so happens that I have two tickets for the concert you were discussing. Unfortunately I can't use them." He paused and looked from one to the other. "Er, may I join you?" he said, smiling. He sat down at their table before they could answer, and introduced himself, "Konstantin Arbelov. I'm staying here at Hintlesham Hall on business. My colleague and I had planned to go to the concert, but sadly we've been called back to London and we must leave the day before it takes place. As we already have the tickets and won't be able to use them, I wondered if you two would accept them? I presume you are staying here?"

Asil said, "Well, no, actually. We only came in for lunch, we're just friends. It's very kind of you Mr Arbelov, such a shame that you have to miss it. I'm sure we'd love to take you up on that." She turned to Luke. "If that's OK, Luke?" He nodded approval. "By the way, I'm Asil Daniels and this is Luke Lomax, a very good friend of mine."

Arbelov took Asil's proffered hand, kissed it lightly and then shook Luke's hand firmly, turning back to a blushing Asil.

"Asil Daniels? Asil is such a pretty and unusual name. This is surely too much of a coincidence, but I knew a Bill Daniels once who also had a daughter named Asil. That couldn't be you by any chance?"

Asil's eyes widened with incredulity. "Well, that's extraordinary! Yes, that's right, I *am* his daughter. Did you know my father then?"

"Why yes. I met him in the Ukraine many years ago, on more than one occasion. It must have been just after you were born I think. I remember that he was so proud of you. The name Asil stuck in my memory.

"The last time we met he described your house so vividly, I can still picture it in my mind. He had never opened up before in such detail. I suspected then that something was bothering him deep down. Almost as if he had a premonition about what might happen in the future."

Arbelov paused, then carried on, "He told me how much you loved your dog, a Springer spaniel, wasn't it?"

"Yes, that's right, his name was Patch and I did love him. We spent hours playing together, he never got tired of chasing sticks and bringing them back, then we'd have a tug of war!"

"And he also described your garden. Your mother loved flowers, I believe."

"Yes, she would often be out weeding and watering until it was almost dark, completely oblivious of the time."

Although Asil was smiling, Arbelov noticed a tear slowly descending down her cheek.

"Oh forgive me, I didn't mean to upset you."

Asil quickly wiped her eye with a tissue.

"No, please go on. I'm sorry but it's bringing back such happy memories, it's a bit overwhelming. *Please* go on."

"Well, perhaps I've said enough for the moment, Asil. You don't mind if I call you Asil?"

"No of course not."

He looked at his watch, stood up and said, "Listen, unfortunately I must leave now for an appointment. If you live locally, perhaps I may drop the tickets off to you, my colleague has them and I won't be seeing him until late this evening."

"Well, if that's not too much trouble. I live in Monks Eleigh, just a few miles from here."

"Give me your address and I'll get them to you tomorrow if that's convenient. Say about 11? It would be nice to have a chat about old times spent with your father."

"That will be fine, Mr Arbelov."

Asil wrote down her address including her mobile phone number and gave it to him.

"It's been a pleasure to meet you both. Till tomorrow, then?"

"We'll look forward to it, wont we, Luke?"

Asil and Luke stood up and Arbelov shook their hands and left.

The two of them sat for a couple of minutes more and finished their drinks. Asil was on a high and said, "Well, Luke, was that *too* much of a coincidence or wasn't it? I can hardly *believe* it! He seemed a really nice man, though. Did you see how he kissed my hand? How chivalrous!"

She knew that Luke was a little jealous and enjoyed teasing him. "It was so kind of him to offer us those tickets. Do you think we should offer to pay him for them?" Asil said.

"I think we should offer, yes. Doesn't look like he's short of money though, does it? Expensively dressed I noticed. Speaks very good English and hardly a trace of an accent. When was your father in the Ukraine then? Did he travel abroad often?"

"He worked for the Foreign Office Luke, I *told* you. He spent most of my childhood travelling all over Europe and even to Japan and China. I better warn Mrs Wade that we're going to have a visitor tomorrow. Can you come too, Luke?"

"I think I better. I don't know that I trust him. Though I don't particularly want to sit and listen to tales about your father's past." Luke's tone was slightly peevish.

"Oh Luke, I really *would* like your support, I'll be embarrassed on my own. Anyway, it'll give us an opportunity to suss him out, won't it?" she said.

"OK, if you really want me to. You know you can twist me round your little finger!"

Luke paid the bill for the lunch on his credit card and they went out to the car. Asil opened the door and was about to get in when she stopped dead.

"*Luke, look!*" She pointed across the car park. The nose of a dark blue Audi was just visible protruding from the other side of some bushes that hid a part of the parking area.

"Isn't that the car we're looking for?" she whispered.

Luke got in beside her. He pulled the piece of paper with the registration number of the Audi written down and confirmed that indeed it was.

"*Now* do you trust this Mr Arbelov? Bowen, Arbelov, are they the same do you think?"

"No, Luke. That definitely wasn't Bowen's voice. I'm going back in. We need to sort this out," said Asil and opened the car door. Luke grabbed her arm firmly.

"No. Stay here. Let's wait a minute or two and see if he comes out to the car. They can't see us from here, but we'll be able to see whoever it is when the car pulls out."

It was some time before the car moved. As it came slowly into view the driver looked left and right and drove slowly up the driveway towards the main road. It was definitely not Arbelov. The man was, as much of him as they could see, broad shouldered and thick necked, probably not that tall, grey haired.

"Aged about 50, would you say?" asked Asil.

Before Luke could answer, another car pulled out and accelerated out of the drive.

"*That* was Arbelov!" shouted Asil. "Quick, let's follow him!"

"*No*. That's madness, Asil. You'd never keep up with him. Anyway, which one are we to follow? Are they together do you think? Or maybe Arbelov is following Bowen. Or perhaps it's just coincidence that they both left together."

"Oh Luke, this is *so* confusing." She frowned and banged her fist on the steering wheel in frustration.

"Look, let's go back home. I'll ring John Nolloth and tell him what's happened."

"Wait a minute," said Luke, "I'm going to go into reception and find out which room Arbelov is staying in. When I come back, you can go in and ask for Bowen's room number. They won't know that we're together."

"And just what will that tell us?" asked Asil.

"Well, they may be sharing a room or have adjoining rooms. If they don't, well…I don't know, but it may tell us *something*."

"Mmm, perhaps you're right. OK, go on then."

Fortunately, the receptionist was a different girl to the one who had been on duty earlier when they had arrived. Luke asked her if he could speak to Mr Arbelov. She looked in the register and without being asked said, "Ah, room 12, just a moment." She looked behind her at the rack that held the room keys. "Sorry sir, he appears to have gone out. Would you like to leave a message?"

"No, I was hoping to see him today. Perhaps I'll try again later in the week. He's not leaving soon, is he?"

She consulted the register again.

"No, he's booked until Thursday. Shall I tell him you called?"

"No. That's not necessary; perhaps I'll ring him this evening. Anyway, thanks for your help."

Luke returned to the car.

"Wow, result! He's staying until Thursday, so he was right about leaving before the concert."

"Great, Luke. How did you wheedle that information out of her then?"

"Just my natural charm! And luckily it's not the same receptionist as the one we saw when we arrived," he said smiling.

"Do you think she'll fall for that twice running though?"

"Try it Asil. What have we got to lose? But let's wait for 15 minutes or so. It might not look so suspicious then."

Twenty minutes later, Asil got back in the car. She was flushed and excited. She smiled at Luke.

"I'm not used to being deceptive, Luke. I was so *nervous*! I'm sure she suspected something. I think she recognized us being together as we left after the meal. Anyway, it doesn't matter. Bowen is staying indefinitely apparently. And he booked in two days before the funeral in Wales. I don't know where that puts us though. What do you think?"

"Hmm, doesn't prove anything one way or the other, really. Come on, let's go and ring your friend Nolloth and bring him up to date."

Asil parked the car in the drive at home and Luke followed her into the house. Mrs Wade was upstairs ironing and Belynda had gone out for the day. Asil went straight through to the drawing room and picked up the phone, while Luke slumped into an armchair. Then she remembered that Nolloth had said not to contact him on the landline, so she put the phone down and used her mobile instead. Nolloth was intrigued when he heard Asil's news.

"Konstantin Arbelov? Mentioned meeting your father in the Ukraine, eh? I suspect that's where he operates from then. I can make inquiries. I don't like this possible connection with Bowen, though. I think it was indiscreet of you to have been so open with him, Asil. The whole meeting at the restaurant must have been contrived, I'm sure of that. I wouldn't advise any more contact with him until I've done a bit of research. I'll get on to it straight away."

"Oh dear, John. Unfortunately I agreed to him coming round to see us in the morning, to bring the tickets for the concert. How can I put him off?"

Nolloth paused for thought. "Look, I'll try and sort something out. Don't do anything to put him off before you hear from me. I do have some more information for you, though. Solvers have recently been dealing with a man named Ion Campeanu. That name sounds very Romanian, doesn't it? I'm looking for information about him at this very moment. Listen, wait till I contact you again before you talk to anyone else outside your friends, OK?"

"I consider my wrist well and truly slapped, John. I'll look forward to your call, and thanks again."

Nolloth rang back that evening.

"You can discount any danger from Konstantin Arbelov. He's working for SIS. Better known as MI6? It may well be that he's onto Bowen, but I can't be sure of that, there are limits to what information I'm allowed into. More importantly, I've unearthed something that might or might not be more sinister. Ion Campeanu arrived from Romania two days before your uncle's death. He met up with Bowen in Aberdovey as soon as he arrived. Apparently they stayed at the same hotel."

Asil interrupted, alarmed, "What are you implying John?"

"I'm not implying anything, Asil. I just think it's a little odd that they arrived with an obvious interest in your inheritance and Gordon Bancroft dies unexpectedly shortly afterwards."

"John, you're frightening me now. These people are close by. At least we know that Bowen is. What can we do without any evidence against them?"

"Asil, I'm going to contact Arbelov. I'm sure he's well aware of what's going on or he wouldn't have made contact with you. That was no coincidence, as I said. Sit tight until you hear from me. If Arbelov contacts you before I've spoken to him, just play it cool and don't let on that you know who he's working for."

Luke was concerned when Asil told him of her conversation with John Nolloth.

"Luke, do you think you could stay here with me for a few days? I'd feel much safer that way. We have a spare room, you won't have to sleep with Mahari," she teased.

"Well, that's a relief! Hmm, I don't know, though."

"Oh, *please* Luke, I'm frightened. What if they murdered Uncle Gordon?"

"Now you're being hysterical, Asil. I'm sure that's very unlikely, the post mortem would have found something, wouldn't they? But you're right, though. Alright, I'll go home and tell my mother that I'll be staying here for a few days. I'll bring some overnight things. Will Mrs Wade mind?"

"No, of course not. She likes you, Luke, and Belynda will be pleased too. And thanks!"

After Luke had left, Asil felt deflated. Here she was, alone, and all dressed up ready for a romantic afternoon and evening and the bad news from John Nolloth had spoilt it all. Oh well, at least Luke had agreed to stay for a few days.

Luke came back that evening with an overnight bag. He apologised for taking so long but said he had a lot of loose ends to tie up regarding his business, in view of not being there for the rest of the week. Mrs Wade showed him up to the room that she'd prepared earlier for him. The spare room was small but comfortable, and Luke was just pleased to be in the same house as Asil.

****

Arbelov was taken by surprise when Nolloth phoned him and asked him outright what was going on, particularly when Nolloth appeared to know that he worked for SIS.

"You are very forthright, Mr Nolloth. I will want some proof of your credentials before I discuss anything at all with you. I'm certainly not pleased that you've contacted me directly. I'll need to check this out."

"Of course. But don't waste my time. Asil Daniels is very dear to me. I suspect, as I'm sure you do, that she could be in some danger. Just get back to me as soon as you can, Arbelov. We need to nail Bowen and this man Campeanu."

Arbelov made a call to his superior in London. He made it plain that he was not happy with Nolloth's interference on the case. His superior assured him that Nolloth had worked on the odd occasion for SIS before and was perfectly capable and trustworthy. He had prior knowledge of the Daniels case and could be very useful, and that he should cooperate with him fully. He said, "Leave it for half an hour or so, Arbelov. I'll get onto Nolloth straight away and smooth things out, OK?"

Arbelov left it an hour before he phoned Nolloth back.

"Nolloth, Arbelov here. We need to talk. I want you down here in Suffolk as soon as possible so that we can discuss this case. Can you make it tomorrow?"

"Your boss gave me a right dressing down, Arbelov. Sorry if I upset you. Sometimes it's the only way to get things done in this world."

Arbelov chuckled. "My dear Nolloth, let's make a fresh start, shall we? I take it that you *will* make it tomorrow, then?"

"It's been made quite plain that I should give you all my support. Yes, I'll leave early in the morning and be with you around midday. Book me a room at your hotel, will you? On your account, OK?"

The man's audacity made Arbelov chuckle.

"No, I don't think that's a good idea. I happen to be keeping an eye on Bowen, that's why I'm staying at Hintlesham Hall. I don't want him to connect the two of us. I'll book you into the Holiday Inn in Ipswich, it's just off the A12, easy to find. I'll meet you in the bar there, OK? But don't tell Miss Daniels that you're coming down just yet. We need to talk first. I'm going to see her tomorrow morning but I should be able to make it to the Holiday Inn by just after lunch, say around two o'clock. I don't want her to know that you will be down here until after I've talked to her."

"Hmm, not sure about that. She needs a bit of reassurance, don't you think?"

"I agree, but not yet. Just do as I say for now, alright?"

Nolloth wasn't used to taking orders but realized that he would have to accept the situation for the present.

"OK. See you tomorrow then."

Arbelov hung up and sat back in his chair. He quite looked forward to meeting this man Nolloth.

Arbelov arrived at Asil's house at 11 the following morning. Mrs Wade answered the door.

"You must be Mr Arbelov," she said smiling "Asil's expecting you. Come in, she and Luke are waiting for you."

She ushered him into the large drawing room where she had already laid out cups and saucers, plates and a plate full of biscuits. Arbelov beamed at Asil and Luke and shook both their hands.

"I don't want to impose on you Miss Daniels. Are you sure I'm not interrupting your plans for the day?"

"Not at all, it's the least we can do as you have so kindly offered us the tickets. May we pay you for them?"

"No, certainly not. I won't hear of it."

He sat in an armchair opposite Asil and Luke.

"I've made some fresh coffee, Mr Arbelov, or would you prefer tea?" asked Mrs Wade.

"Fresh coffee! I could smell it when I came in. That'll be fine."

Asil was anxious to get on with hearing about her father.

"Now Mr Arbelov, tell me about my father. Did you know him well?"

"Not all *that* well, no. We met a few times to discuss business matters. It was in Kiev. We shared a few good meals and more than a few drinks together. It was always a pleasure to deal with Bill; he was so accommodating. It was a difficult time for both our countries but we never let politics get in the way of our relationship regarding business. I believe your mothers name was Carole? He showed me a photograph of her once. She was a very beautiful lady. I think they were very much in love, isn't that right?"

"Yes they were. I miss them both terribly still."

"I'm sure you do. It's such a shame that they died so tragically and so young. I can see that he left you well provided for though. I hope you won't take offence, Asil, but your father was always on the lookout for, shall I say, any extra opportunities for a business deal for himself as well as for the interests of your country. Particularly when he had a beautiful new young daughter to look after! I haven't yet told you, but I ran into him in London shortly before he died. He was very concerned about a deal he had done in Romania that involved some works of art. In fact he confided in me and asked me for advice on handling it. He was most concerned that the authorities should not get wind of it. Are you aware of the facts regarding how he came by the treasure?"

"Oh yes. My uncle, Doctor Bancroft, explained it all to me. I was too young at the time to realize that the deal was bordering on the criminal, although he did intimate that it was not quite above board."

"Well, your father was very concerned for his own safety at the time. So much so that I advised him how he should hide the items concerned. I put him in touch with contact of mine in Japan, a Mr Kurosawa, an electronics genius, and I believe he made a tracking device for your father. Kurosawa told me later on anyway, but didn't give me the details."

"Why yes, it was a silver box, I still have it." Asil stopped herself there. She realised that she shouldn't have given away that information. "I was far too young to have taken in all the consequences. But you're quite right, those art treasures paid for this house and set me up very well for the future."

Arbelov nodded and paused for thought before saying: "Well, I hope you employed a good agent to get the best prices for them. I presume that you managed to sell it all?"

"Oh no, only two or three paintings. The rest are in keeping for me until I'm 21. But I must say that sitting on all that amount of wealth brings problems that I don't particularly need."

"In what way?" asked Arbelov?

"Well, a few years ago, Romanian agents were sent over here to recover some items that my father had left to me. And I believe that attempts are being made again right now."

Arbelov drained the last of his coffee before commenting.

"Look, Asil, here is my card. You can contact me at any time. I have many contacts in the diplomatic world. If I can be of any assistance please let me know. Now I feel I have outstayed my welcome. I really must leave now and thank you so much for your hospitality. I shall be staying at Hintlesham Hall again in a couple of week's time. May I call you then?"

"Please do Mr Arbelov. You'll be very welcome."

After he had left, Luke voiced his fears that Asil had been a little too candid with Mr Arbelov.

"You know nothing about him, Asil. He may well be out to track down the treasure himself. He's certainly a smooth operator."

"No, Luke. I'm sure he's genuine. I have an instinct for this sort of thing. He could turn out to be a great help to us."

"To us?" Luke said smiling.

"Yes, Luke. I rate you as a friend. Someone I can trust and share things with. And I hope you're going to help me through this."

They heard his car start outside and crunch down the gravel drive.

"Just a minute! What about the tickets? He didn't leave them, did he?"

Luke rushed out to the front door just in time to see the silver

Mercedes disappearing down the road.

Arbelov parked a mile down the road outside the village and made a call on his mobile phone to the Regent Theatre. He heaved a sigh of relief when he found that seats were still available for the concert and reserved two. He drove straight into Ipswich and picked up the tickets that he'd just ordered. He put them in an envelope already addressed to Asil and posted it first class at the main post office. He then rang Asil on her mobile and apologized for not leaving the tickets, and told her that they were in the post.

The bar at the Holiday Inn was almost deserted when Nolloth arrived. He looked around and spotted a distinguished looking man wearing an expensive Italian cut suit and reading a newspaper in the corner. He recognized Arbelov from the photo that had been emailed to him that morning. Nolloth ordered a pint of Adnam's and took it over to the table.

"May I join you?" he asked.

Arbelov looked up from his paper to see a rather stocky, shabbily dressed man looking down at him with a pint glass in his hand.

"Mr Nolloth, I presume?"

"The very same," smiled Nolloth, proffering his hand. Arbelov put his newspaper down, stood up and shook his hand firmly. Nolloth sat down opposite him. "Mr Arbelov I presume?"

"That's right"

"Let's skip the pleasantries, Arbelov. Straight down to business, eh? Are you going to tell me what you know about this case and then we'll—"

"Not so fast, Nolloth. I'm enjoying a very fine single malt whisky at the moment and I won't have you spoil the highlight of my day. Now, apart from being an hour late, did you have a pleasant journey?"

"No. I hate driving on motorways. And since you seem reluctant to put me in the picture, I'll start, shall I?" Before Arbelov could protest, Nolloth carried on, "This company called Solvers. I presume you know of them?"

Arbelov nodded that indeed he did.

"Good. It intrigues me that this man Campeanu arrived two days before Bancroft's alleged heart attack. And he met your man Bowen as soon as he arrived. What conclusions do you draw from that?"

Arbelov looked down into his glass, swilled the whisky around and took a sip of it before replying. He was surprised that Nolloth already had so much information. He was impressed.

"You're concluding from that that they may have had something to do with Bancroft's death, I presume?"

"Well, doesn't it sound too much of a coincidence to you?"

Arbelov paused again.

"Campeanu is a suspected assassin in his own country. It is most likely, Nolloth, that either he or Bowen poisoned Bancroft. My intention is to work on Bowen so that we may get enough evidence to have Bancroft's body exhumed. I desperately want to nail Campeanu but he's too clever a man to leave any evidence of his involvement."

"So how do you intend to get Bowen?"

"By allowing him to make a move on Asil Daniels."

"*What?* Are you *serious*? That's outrageous! I won't have you put that girl in danger, Arbelov. She's been through enough in her short life already."

Arbelov sat silently for several seconds studying Nolloth before commenting.

"You disappoint me, Nolloth. I have to leave for a short time on Thursday on another assignment. I intended to leave you in charge."

"To do what, keep an eye on Bowen?"

"Of course. You will be responsible for the Daniels girl's safety."

"Then I'll have to move in to the Hintlesham Hall Hotel as soon as you leave."

"Good, I'll book you in from Thursday evening. That's settled then. Meanwhile, if anything develops before I leave on Thursday I'll let you know."

Nolloth stared at Arbelov, shaking his head.

"Arbelov, you've not told me what it is that Campeanu wants from Asil's inheritance. It can't be just for the value of it. Is there something else hidden within it? Like those incriminating documents that they were after the last time?"

"I wish I knew. We won't really know the answer to that unless we actually catch them in the act. But I'm working on that. That's why we have to be so careful in handling this situation."

Nolloth fell silent while he absorbed this information. Arbelov sipped his whisky patiently, not taking his eyes off Nolloth.

Nolloth said: "OK, now back to the present. I really must let Asil know that I've arrived here. I'll have to tell her that you and I are working together to nail Bowen. I won't mention the threat that he poses. Is that alright?"

"That's reasonable. You must stress that neither she nor her friend Lomax take matters into their own hands. That could be very dangerous for both of them."

"I agree. I know Asil well enough to have every confidence in her ability to handle the situation in a mature way. She may only be nineteen, Arbelov, but she's been through more traumatic experiences than most people encounter in a lifetime, and she's a very intelligent and well balanced girl."

Nolloth began to wonder why he had agreed to join Arbelov. He would have preferred to go it alone. But it was too late now. They agreed to meet again the next evening at the Holiday Inn. Arbelov said his goodbyes and left Nolloth to find his room and settle in.

****

Bowen deeply regretted that he'd fallen in with Ion Campeanu. But the money offered him for his assistance by this Romanian a couple of months previously had been too good to be true, particularly as he had been earning very little since being dismissed from the Foreign Office. He didn't realize at the time that it would involve being an accessory to a murder. Burglary, yes, that was OK by him. Campeanu, a cold, unemotional sadist, actually stood and smiled as Gordon Bancroft collapsed and painfully fought for his last breath after he had been poisoned. And it was Bowen who had lured Bancroft to meeting with Campeanu by professing to know of a plot to abduct the girl Daniels for a second time.

Campeanu had used a tiny hypodermic to inject a substance into Bancroft's arm whilst Bowen held his frail, protesting frame. A substance that Campeanu had insisted would put Bancroft to sleep for a couple of hours while they searched the house. All lies. In fact, it was a poison, deadly, that was almost instantaneous and that he insisted afterwards was virtually undetectable. Once Bancroft had, to Bowen's horror, stopped breathing, Campeanu had laughed and said, "Come Bowen. We'll look for the documents another time." He turned and calmly arranged everything as if nothing had happened and walked out of the house and out to the car. A shocked Bowen picked up Bancroft's walking stick and placed it next to the body and followed Campeanu, shutting the door and wiping his fingerprints off the handle.

Now Bowen was in fear of his life, not knowing how to extricate himself from this situation. He had to follow it through now until the documents were recovered, although he had no idea how that would be accomplished. And then hopefully Campeanu would return to his own country.

Waiting for his next instructions from the Romanian was causing him a great deal of stress.

EXHUMATION AND CREMATION

Arbelov went straight up to Nolloth's room and knocked on the door.

"Who is it?"

"Arbelov."

Almost before the door was fully open Arbelov pushed his way in.

"In a hurry, are we?" said Nolloth.

"Good news, my friend. I have arranged an exhumation on Bancroft's body. So I've bought a bottle of Glenmorangie with me to celebrate. Come on, Nolloth, at least try to look pleased!"

"About the exhumation or the whisky?" said Nolloth smiling, although a bit miffed that this suave Russian could get things done so quickly.

"Glasses, man. Come on!" said Arbelov impatiently.

They settled themselves in armchairs with their drinks.

"So when will it take place?"

"In a couple of days, hopefully. If it reveals what I think it will, we should be able to tackle Bowen. And I have some more information for you. Apparently Campeanu and Bowen had been in contact several weeks before Campeanu came to this country."

"So you think this might have been pre planned then?"

"Possibly. Probably. We lack evidence of their visit to Bancroft's house, but if the autopsy proves that he was murdered then we must find something, surely?"

Nolloth was more cautious. "You're assuming rather a lot, Arbelov. Let's wait and see, shall we?"

"If we do need evidence, Nolloth, it will be down to you to find it. It's on your patch after all. Be a bit more optimistic, man! Now I really must go." He emptied his glass and put it down on the table and stood up. "You can finish the bottle if you like, I've got to drive. I'll let you know as soon as I hear the results of the autopsy. I think you better get yourself back to Wales tomorrow and get ready to start searching Bancroft's house as soon as I give the word."

"What about Bowen? I'm supposed to be protecting Asil from him."

"You're a bit late, John. Bowen left this morning, handed in his hire car and bought a single train ticket to London."

Nolloth was beginning to feel inadequate. This man Arbelov was miles in front of every move that was being made.

****

Jake Bull downed his fourth pint in the Morton Arms in Towyn. At last he could start to spend his earnings for his part in the Bancroft affair. Bowen had warned him to be doubly careful until after the autopsy on the doctor. Now Bull felt relieved that no charge of accessory to murder could fall on him after the verdict of death by natural causes had been passed.

He was a big man and a bully. He delighted in being the centre of attention with his cronies in the pub, when he had enough money to buy them drinks. This night he was forcing his attention on Carter Thomas, another of the men that were sent down for his part in the murder of Asil's parents ten years ago, in which Jake Bull had been an accessory and served time. After the fifth pint, Jake Bull's voice was becoming a little slurred, and louder.

"Let me tell you something, Carter." He put his arm around Carter's shoulder and breathed his beery breath in his ear. "Let me tell you something really funny, boyo. You know what? I got paid for a burglary, Carter!" He laughed out loud then put his finger to his lips and looked around before whispering, "A burglary. Old Bancroft's place, remember him? And I didn't take nothin', see boy! Did you ever hear of anythin' so bloody funny? Paid for burglin' and we didn't take a thing!" He burst out laughing again and banged Thomas's shoulder with his fist, staggered a bit and picked up his glass. "Have another one on me, boyo!"

Carter turned away in disgust. He didn't like Bull and he had no wish to get involved with anything that he'd done.

"No thanks, Jake. Look, I must be off now, see. Thanks for the drink, though. See you tomorrow perhaps, eh?"

Carter Thomas walked out into the car park. It was dark and a light rain was falling, creating a mist that Carter had to wipe from the car windows before getting in. He started it and reversed out, cleared the windscreen with his wipers. As he went to pull forward a man stepped out of the darkness and stood in front of his bonnet and held up his hand. Thomas stopped. The man walked to the passenger door, opened it and stooped to look in. The man smiled.

"Don't be alarmed, Mr Thomas. I just want to talk to you for a moment, is that alright?" He eased himself into the seat without being invited.

He wore a black bobble hat pulled over his ears and down to his eyebrows. He pulled down the scarf that covered his mouth. Broad shoulders and a slim waist suggested an athletic build. He moved very easily.

"You're a friend of Mr Bull, I think?"

"Not exactly. Why do you ask?" said Carter Thomas irritably, annoyed at the man's intrusion.

"Oh, let's just say that I have an interest in his welfare, shall we?"

Carter sneered and said, "You look like a policeman to me."

The man laughed quietly and said:

"Yes, you might think that, Mr Thomas. But it's Mr Bull I'm interested in, not you. I happen to know that you are still on parole Mr Thomas, that's right, isn't it? So please answer my questions truthfully. Now, what was it that you discussed with him just now in the pub?"

Carter turned to study the man, puzzled now and growing more apprehensive by the second. He hadn't seen the man in the pub, so how did he know about their conversation? Must have been looking through the window, he presumed. He turned away to look out of the windscreen which was already misting up inside. He wiped it away with his hand.

"I didn't discuss nothin'. *He* discussed with *me*. Somethin' about a burglary that he didn't get nothin' out of. As if I'm interested. I don't want to get mixed up with anythin' Bull has a hand in, see. Not any more."

"Is that all he said? Did he say where this alleged burglary took place?"

Thomas hesitated. "Look, Jake Bull is a violent man. I don't want to get on the wrong side of him."

The man said, "Look at me, Thomas. You would be well advised to think about your answer." Carter became aware of the sudden menace in this man's voice. "I don't want to make this difficult for you, but I can easily have you back in prison."

"OK! OK. He said it was the Bancroft place."

The man nodded as if that was what he expected to hear. He smiled and faced away from Carter. His voice softened and his smile returned.

"Good, Mr Thomas. That's very good. Thank you. You won't hear any more from me, *but* .....only if you forget that we have had this conversation. Do you understand?"

"Yes. Yes, I understand. Now I just want to keep out of trouble and get home, right?"

The man got out of the car, leaned back in and said, "Not a word, Mr Thomas. Or..." He drew his finger across his neck from ear to ear and then pointed it at Carter Thomas ominously. "Goodnight."

The man stood there in the dark, slammed the car door shut and watched as Carter drove off with wheels spinning. He removed his bobble hat and scarf, smoothed his hair back and smiled to himself.

Jake Bull was slumped on the bar, leaning on his elbows. He was glaring at the barman.

"So you won't let me have another drink then, George? Well you better look out when you leave off then. I'll be waitin' for you outside, see boyo?"

George glared at him and continued wiping glasses. "You've had too much already, Jake. Be sensible and go home, man."

Jake got up and walked unsteadily to the door, turned and spat in the direction of the bar, raised two fingers and went out into the dark to start the short walk home. He stumbled on the uneven shingle in the car park and almost fell. He felt a steadying arm round his shoulder. "Steady on old chap, nearly went over then! Let me give you a hand, eh?" Jake Bull shook himself free and glared at his rescuer.

"Who the hell are you?" he growled ungraciously.

The man said, smiling, "Just a friend, Mr Bull, just a friend."

Jake steadied himself and peered into the strangers smiling face for a few seconds. He wasn't used to being called Mr Bull.

"Wouldn't let me 'ave another drink, that miserable sod. All the money I spend here and he wouldn't let me 'ave just one more drink." He stood swaying and regarding this supposed new friend suspiciously.

"Don't worry Mr Bull, I've got a good bottle of whisky I'll share with you if you like. Come on, I've got a little proposition for you. Let's get away from this unfriendly place shall we?"

The man pulled a bottle of whisky from inside his jacket.

"Now, old chap, my place is across the road, I've got a lot more drink there. Come and share it with me, eh?"

Jake made a grab for the bottle with one hand and pushed the man away with the other, and said, "Not so fast, you." He removed the top and took a long swig while swaying on his feet. The man pulled on a pair of gloves and took hold of Jake's arm.

"You can keep the bottle. Better to drink it in comfort, though." He manoeuvred the big man across the road and into a holiday caravan park. It was dark but the man found his way to a small caravan. He opened the door and pushed Jake up the step and into the caravan. Jake slumped onto the settee and took another long swig from the bottle, took a cigarette from a packet in his pocket and lit it with difficulty with a match from a box he pulled from his pocket.

The man opened a cupboard and took out another bottle and glass and poured himself a drink. He stood watching Jake slowly finish the bottle that he refused to leave his grasp. Bull seemed oblivious to the man's presence, muttering to himself about what he was going to do to George the barman. Soon sleep overtook him and he subsided onto the settee, one leg dangling over the side, and began to snore loudly. The man stared down at him and smiled to himself. He put his almost full bottle down beside the empty one by the settee where Jakes hand hung close to the floor. He gently closed Jakes fingers around the bottle and then let the contents empty onto the carpet. He lit one of Jake's matches and set fire to the spilled whisky, picked up the empty bottle and his own glass and retreated hastily out of the door as the carpet burst into flames. The inside of the caravan was lit by a blazing inferno in a matter of seconds. He heard Jake Bull coughing and stumbling about inside while the man held the door tight shut. The handle quickly became too hot to hold even in his gloved hand. He let go and ran just as an explosion ripped the caravan apart.

****

Arbelov didn't like being kept waiting when he arrived at Lloyd, Lloyd & Carraghers and it showed. He refused a coffee offered by the secretary and he paced up and down agitatedly, while the secretary typed, nervously stealing an occasional look at him. At last her phone buzzed. She answered it and said to Arbelov, "You may go in now, Mr. Arbelov." He smiled, nodded and walked purposefully into Mr Lloyd Junior's office.

"Now Mr Arbelov, what can I do for you?"

Arbelov produced an official letter from his pocket and handed it to Mr Lloyd.

Lloyd studied it, frowned and looked up at Arbelov.

"I'm not in agreement with your department's request, but I see that there's not much I can do to stop you. Although I have to tell you that your journey has been wasted Mr Arbelov. The items that you wish to inspect are in fact in a bank vault in London. I took the opportunity to contact the Reverend Anthony O'Malley after your initial phone call and he kindly, but reluctantly, opened the Bancroft briefcase and supplied the information."

Arbelov smiled and said, "I appreciate your co-operation Mr Lloyd. I know that this is difficult for you, but it is in the interest of Miss Daniels and I can assure you that anything we may, er, disturb in the course of our investigation, will be returned to its original condition. If you would prefer to have one of your representatives to be present then that will be perfectly acceptable."

Lloyd didn't like any form of authority being exercised over his rights as a solicitor and he didn't particularly like the smooth and rather superior manner in which Arbelov conducted himself.

"That won't be necessary Mr Arbelov, I'll have to trust you and the SIS to conduct the operation in a professional manner. I have contacted the bank and they are expecting your call. I presume that that is all?"

Arbelov gave a low chuckle and held out his hand. "You have been most accommodating Mr Lloyd. I thank you on behalf of Miss Daniels, though she knows nothing of this operation and I would be most grateful if she is not made aware of it. I am sure I can trust you on this?"

"You have my word, Mr Arbelov."

Lloyd handed him a piece of paper with the bank details regarding the vault. Arbelov thanked him and headed for the door before stopping and turning to face Lloyd.

"Just one more thing, Mr Lloyd. As far as we know, the people involved do not know that your firm holds the Daniels will or the whereabouts of the bank vault. If they do find out, they may try to recover it from you, or at least find out where the treasure is being held. I do hope the security of this building is up to scratch. If it isn't, I suggest you do something about it pretty quickly. And if you have any contact with anyone seeking such information, either physically or by phone, that you feel is suspicious, contact me immediately, for your own safety. Goodbye."

He left Lloyd open mouthed and apprehensive, and left before he could reply.

****

Asil was not shocked at the news when Nolloth told her that the Romanians were once more after information from her. She had suspected as much from the moment Bowen had threatened her. Luke was shocked though, and concerned regarding Asil's safety.

"Luke, don't worry. I have absolute faith in John Nolloth. If I were in any immediate danger he would tell me. We'll just have to be patient and see what Arbelov comes up with. Any way, I feel safe while you're around."

Asil's life had been devoid of any real love since her parents had been murdered. From being thoroughly spoilt by her loving parents she had been passed to an insane aunt, who hated and abused her, then threatened her with torture before being rescued and deposited with Marjorie Wade and her daughter Belynda. Mrs Wade was very kind and motherly, but it wasn't the same as being loved as her parents had loved her. And if that wasn't trauma enough, a year later she was kidnapped, bound and gagged, driven half way across the country not knowing what her fate was to be before she was rescued once again.

It was not surprising then that Asil had developed a carapace of diffidence that made it difficult for others to interpret her moods or to get very close to her emotionally during the following years. Although she was outwardly confident, she was very wary about making friends or getting too involved with people. As the years passed, she had become more outgoing but hadn't made any really close friends. Her personality mirrored that of her mother's, and she echoed her good looks and figure. Although people were attracted to her, she hadn't been able to react to it. The last three years had been exciting for her, though. Gordon Bancroft had allowed her access to her finances so that she could take driving lessons. She took to driving like a duck to water and passed her driving test at the first attempt. Choosing her first car was a great thrill, and then when she reached her 18th birthday her uncle suggested that she bought her own house. Asil decided to move to Suffolk where she had taken refuge years ago before she was abducted. Her uncle helped her to choose where she wanted to live and they searched the estate agents for a suitable home. It was Asil's decision to have the Wades live with her, something that Uncle Gordon thoroughly approved of. Choosing the furnishings was left entirely to Asil and both Mrs Wade and Gordon Bancroft were amazed at her mature and artistic taste.

Asil's growing relationship with Luke had surprised her. For the first time she had a male companion she could trust and perhaps grow to love. Oh, she'd had a few so-called boyfriends through school and college, but none had been able to get really close to her. Always on the defensive, she was unable to trust any of them. But now she felt an increasing *frisson* of excitement every time she and Luke met. She needed to feel strong arms around her and to have a sympathetic voice whispering kind thoughts in her ear.

John Nolloth had been busy. On re-examining the evidence still contained within the Bancroft house, fingerprints had been found on Bancroft's walking stick. Because it had been thought that death was due to natural causes, the local police had failed to pursue this avenue of investigation. And better still, he had a match for the fingerprints. Charles Bowen's. The results of the exhumation of Bancroft's body were now hastened, and as soon as the results were known and if they confirmed that his death was not natural, he could have Bowen arrested. Arbelov was delighted at the news, and congratulated Nolloth on his diligence. "The sooner we have Bowen out of circulation, the safer it will be for Asil," said Arbelov. "But we must remember that Bowen is not working alone. Unless we can find a link with Campeanu, we can't be sure that this is over."

"Another puzzle has emerged, Arbelov. I noticed that in the local press here in Towyn, that a body had been found in a burnt-out holiday caravan. Dental records have confirmed that the deceased is no other than Jake Bull. The man that was goaled for his part in the murder of Asil's parents."

Arbelov raised his eyebrows in surprise.

"What do the police make of it John, do you know?"

"Only that apparently the caravan was not rented by Bull, but by a Mr Scott, who paid cash to rent it for a week. The fire happened a day after the rental started, and the details that Scott gave are false. Although he did produce an electricity bill when asked for identification, the address on it was non-existent. Obviously forged. So it has all the hallmarks of a pre-meditated murder."

"Can you pursue this further, or are the police not happy to have you on the case?"

"I'm on to it already. There was another man involved with Jake Bull for the same crime that Bull was jailed for, a local man by the name of Carter Thomas. He was released from prison on parole recently. I'll follow that up and keep you posted. The police here have very limited resources and it could be days before they get anywhere with the investigation."

"Good, John. Meanwhile, I'll try and trace Campeanu's movements. This sounds like just the kind of thing he would have been involved in."

Having Luke staying at the house was working out well. Both Mrs Wade and Belynda adored him, and Asil was happy to have his company and the benefit of the extra security that he provided. The fact that they had heard nothing from John Nolloth for a few days tended to push the danger to the back of their minds, especially as they were enjoying a spell of warm and sunny June weather. Asil took time off from the charity office in Ipswich and over the next few days Mrs Wade packed a picnic for Asil and Luke that they ate by the river in Hadleigh. During that week they watched cricket on Castle Park in Colchester, hired a rowing boat in Dedham, rowed to Flatford and visited Willy Lots cottage, and spent an evening at the jazz club in Stoke-by-Nayland. Asil was enjoying Luke's company, and the more time she spent with him the more she realised that she was falling in love with him.

When Nolloth finally did make contact, it brought the full danger of the situation to the forefront once again.

Asil was horrified to hear of the death of Jake Bull, not so much because of his death, she loathed the man, but because it brought back all too vividly the circumstances of the murder of her parents. She had not been aware that Carter Thomas, also involved, had been released from jail and was living in Towyn. After John's phone call, Asil related all the details to Luke. She was almost hysterical at the thought that whoever was responsible for Jake Bull's murder was at large and that it was related somehow to her inheritance. He had never seen her so upset, never witnessed her losing control in that way and it concerned him greatly. Luke insisted that she had a stiff drink and calmed down. He tried to persuade her that if there was any imminent danger then Nolloth or Arbelov would sort it out. She felt better after that and apologized for her behaviour, cuddling up to him on the sofa as she used to with her father when she was young. The events of the past few days were having more of an effect on her mental health than she had realized.

That night she couldn't sleep as dark thoughts of Jake Bull and Carter Thomas flooded her mind. She tossed and turned, recalling the worst moments of her abduction and ill treatment by Alexandrou and Vasiliu, the two Romanian agents who had kidnapped her all those years ago. Someone, a long time ago, had told her that the best way to get to sleep was to close your eyes, focus them on a point in the middle of your forehead, then imagine a wave of relaxation descending downwards over your body. Starting with relaxing every muscle in your face, then neck, chest, abdomen and gradually down to your toes until every bit of tension had been taken from your body. She at last fell into a deep sleep.

She saw in the pitch black a small pinpoint of red. It seemed to be edging towards her very slowly, getting larger as it did so. It was a glowing ember. Closer it came and closer still. She began to make out the silhouette of a face above it that gradually took shape. Long, matted grey hair, wide staring eyes, and a malevolent smile. She recognised her insane aunt Morag holding a red-hot soldering iron about to plunge it into her forehead. She could feel the heat now and screamed...

Asil awoke, sweating, her throat dry. She didn't know if she had indeed screamed out aloud.

It took a few seconds before her heart returned to its normal beat. She turned on the bedside light and looked at the clock. She sighed when she saw that it was only just after 2am and she'd hardly slept a wink.

She remembered all too vividly how in real life, Jake Bull forced her into a chair and tied her to it in Morag Flynn's cottage. She remembered biting his arm and drawing blood and the smell of his sweaty unwashed body. She could see Jake heating a soldering iron on the gas ring until it glowed red and passing it to her aunt, and relived again the terror of knowing what was about to happen to her. She shuddered and realised that she didn't really care that Jake Bull had met his end.

Her thoughts turned back to her childhood. When, after suffering a nightmare, she'd crept into her parents' bed for her mother to comfort her.

She slipped out of bed, pulled on a negligee, turned off the light, and tiptoed out onto the landing and silently into Luke's room. She stood just inside the door and when her eyes had adjusted to the darkness she could see that he was sound asleep, lying on his side with one arm dangling over the edge of the bed. She slid in beside him and cuddled up to his back, kissing him gently on the back of his neck. He stirred and felt Asil's warm body pressing against him. He turned to face her and she was soon enveloped in his welcoming arms.

At breakfast, Mrs Wade and Belynda exchanged knowing glances while Asil and Luke smiled at each other as they touched feet under the table. Mahari just looked bored and munched noisily on his toast.

CARTER THOMAS

Nolloth knocked on Carter Thomas's door and waited. No one came. He peered through the window into the living room and spotted a steaming mug on the coffee table. He banged hard once again on the door and shouted through the letterbox:

"I know you're in there, Carter. It's John Nolloth. I'm not the police any more, but they may well be here soon if you don't talk to me."

After a few seconds the door was unlocked and an unshaven Carter Thomas opened the door a crack.

"What do you want, Mr Nolloth?"

"Just to talk. May I come in?"

Thomas grunted and opened the door.

"Your friend Jake Bull came to a sticky end, then. Do you—"

"He wasn't my friend, I didn't have anythin' to do with it."

"You were drinking in the pub with him the night he died, though."

"I wasn't drinkin' with him really. He came in and brought me a drink or two. He was rabittin' on about a burglary he'd helped with, I didn't want to know anythin' about it, see."

Thomas was agitated and his hands were shaking. He moved over to the sideboard and took out a bottle of rum and poured a good measure into his coffee cup and took a swig.

"Was that all? Did you stay in the pub with him? Did you leave with him?"

"No I didn't. He offered me another drink but I didn't want to get involved. He was pretty well pissed anyway. I left him as soon as I'd finished my drink."

“So you went straight home did you?”

“Yes, I went straight home.”

“Well, the landlord’s wife said she was looking out of the bedroom window and saw a man stop your car and get in with you.”

Nolloth waited to see the reaction to this.

Thomas took another mouthful from his coffee cup and added more rum. He rubbed his unshaven face with both hands and began shaking his head.

“Well, is this true Carter?”

“Look Mr Nolloth, I’m on parole, I don’t want to go back to prison again.” He was whining now. “Please, I can’t say no more.”

Nolloth got up from his chair. “Right then Carter, I don’t suppose it’ll be long before the local police come calling. I’ll leave it to them, then, shall I? I can’t help you if you won’t tell me the truth.”

Thomas was close to tears.

“It was nothin’, really. This man wanted to know what Jake had been sayin’ to me. I didn’t *want* to tell him, but he got nasty and threatened me, so I told him that it was about burglin’ the Bancroft house. He threatened to cut my throat if I told anyone I’d spoken to him.”

“Who was this man, did you know him?”

“Never seen ’im before in me life, I swear. He ’ad a bit of a foreign accent though.”

“So what did he look like?”

“It was dark, I couldn’t really see. He had a bobble hat on, pulled well down like, and a scarf over ’is mouth. Quite tall though. That’s all, really.”

“And what happened then?”

“I drove off and left him in the car park.”

“Was Jake still in the pub?”

“I s’pose so, I ’adn’t seen him come out.”

"Had you noticed this man in the pub while you were in there?"

"I don't think so, I 'adn't seen him before."

Nolloth was puzzled but he believed Thomas. He was obviously a very frightened man. Nolloth got up and went to the door.

"Aren't you goin' to 'elp me then, Mr Nolloth?"

"If I were you, Carter, I'd go away and stay with friends or relations for a while."

He left and shut the door behind him.

Arbelov was quite excited when he heard Nolloth's report of his meeting with Carter Thomas.

"The description given by Carter Thomas could be of anybody, but I bet that it was Ion Campeanu. And Jake Bull's murder has his stamp all over it. We must find this man and quickly. Now we know to what lengths he'll go to, Asil is in even more danger than we thought."

"Do we have any idea as to his movements?" asked Nolloth.

"None, I'm afraid. The next we'll hear of him is when he makes his next move, and we'll just have to hope that it's not on Asil."

KIDNAP

Walter Lloyd lived above the offices of Lloyd, Lloyd and Carraghers in a large apartment that occupied two of the four floors of the Victorian building. It was tastefully furnished, largely with antique pieces bought by his father many years before his death. Walter lived a quiet, happy life with his wife Tamsin who was a consultant at the hospital in Aberystwyth. She had an apartment there close to the hospital that saved her travelling the 30-odd mile journey daily.

Walter was in the habit of taking a walk after closing the office, usually along the sea front, clearing his head after a day spent in his rather stuffy office.

He was standing this particular evening, drinking in the sea air and watching the sun reflect off the water when he was aware of a man standing a few feet away and staring at him. As their eyes met, the other man turned away and fixed his eyes on the sea, saying "A beautiful evening, Mr Lloyd."

"Yes, I never get tired of this view, whatever the weather. It acts as a full stop to my day," he said, smiling. "I'm sorry, I can't place you. Do we know each other?"

"Only by sight. I happened to be waiting in your lobby one day some time ago when you were seeing Doctor Bancroft, an old friend of mine. He's dead, you know. Died suddenly of a heart attack quite recently."

"Ah, I see. Yes, I did know."

"Did you handle his affairs, Mr Lloyd?"

"Ah, that's confidential information, I'm afraid."

“I’ll take that as a yes, then. I need to know the whereabouts of certain items acquired by a William Daniels and entrusted to your care, I believe?”

“I’ve already told you—”

The man moved closer to him and grasped his upper arm in an iron grip.

“I don’t care what you’ve told me that you can’t do, Mr Lloyd, I’ll tell you what I can do, shall I?”

Lloyd was alarmed now. The man’s attitude was very threatening. He looked up and down the sea front, but there was hardly a soul in sight. The man was hurting him now. He tried to shake free.

“I wouldn’t think of doing anything silly now, Mr Lloyd. Let’s take a walk to your house, shall we, and we can discuss this matter in a civilised way. Just in case you should be foolish enough to do anything that might upset me, I also know that your lovely wife won’t be home from the hospital for another two days.”

Lloyd was terrified now. The man had an icy confidence about him. He even knew about his wife’s movements, it seemed. Arbelov’s words of warning had been proved correct. Now Lloyd had to think fast in order not to endanger her.

They arrived at his office. Lloyd opened the door and the man guided him inside. Lloyd led him up to his living room where the man let go of his arm.

“I’m sure you could do with a drink, Mr Lloyd, you look quite pale. Pour me one too, a strong vodka and tonic, I’m sure you have some.”

“I only have whisky, I’m afraid,” Lloyd said as he went to the drinks cabinet and poured himself a whisky and soda, his hands shaking.

“That will do then, a little water with it please. Now down to business. The last will and testament of William Daniels, Mr Lloyd. Where are the items that interest me?”

"I don't know what items you mean. I don't know what you're talking about. I *honestly* don't know. Look, that information was entrusted to a friend by Mr Daniels, the will simply stated that until his daughter reached 21 years of age, that information would remain a secret."

The man smiled, then laughed out loud.

"You expect me to believe that? Do you really think I am that much of a fool?"

He stood up, walked over to Lloyd and struck him forcefully across the face with the back of his hand, drawing blood from Lloyd's lower lip.

"Get me the will Lloyd, now. Get it now, no more messing me around. Think of your wife, Lloyd. Think of her."

Lloyd wiped the blood oozing from his split lip. "It's in my files, downstairs, in the office," he said haltingly, now fearing for his life and not being able to see an immediate way out.

The man followed him down the stairs, a Beretta pistol now in his hand and nudging into Lloyd's back. Lloyd took a bunch of keys from his desk and tried to unlock the filing cabinet, but his hand was shaking so much that he couldn't locate the key in the lock. The man grabbed the keys and opened it himself, then pointed the pistol at the draw and nodded for Lloyd to get the file. The will was snatched from his hand and Lloyd was told to sit down and not move while the man studied it.

"Where is this Reverend Anthony O'Malley?" he asked.

"The Old Rectory, St Martins church, not far away."

"Put the will back. Lock the draw and put the keys back in your desk. We're leaving now."

"Leaving?" said Lloyd nervously.

"Yes, leaving."

Lloyd did as he was told and then was taken out of the office and into the street. He locked the door behind them. He was led to the man's car and told to get in the front passenger seat. The man opened the glove compartment and produced a pair of handcuffs that he applied to Lloyd's wrists. He fastened Lloyd's seat belt and covered his hands with a tartan car blanket. He drove calmly away and out into the country, pulling off the road after some 20 minutes or so into a wood. He got out and told Lloyd to get out and walk in front of him. Lloyd sensed that he was near to death and began to shake.

"It's alright, I'm not going to shoot you, Lloyd. Walk straight ahead along the path."

They came to a wooden hut, the door of which had an iron bar across it with a large padlock attached. The man unlocked it and pushed Lloyd inside. It was furnished with a couple of wooden chairs, a table, a stove and a couple of wall cupboards. It smelt musty and damp.

"Sit," ordered the man. Lloyd sat. He took out some cord and some gaffer tape from the table draw and bound Lloyd's body to the chair. He removed the handcuffs and bound his hands and feet then taped over his mouth with the gaffer tape and left without saying another word, locking the bar across the door. After the man had left, Lloyd struggled to free himself but he was bound too tightly. Tears of frustration welled up in his eyes. He feared for his wife's safety and wondered if he would ever see her again.

CHARLES BOWEN

Charles Bowen heard something drop through his letterbox and hurried down the hall to see what had been delivered. Seven in the morning was unusually early for the post. It was a brown typewritten A6 envelope. Bowen had been on edge since he returned to his flat in Chelsea, not having heard anything from Campeanu. He took it to a chair by the window where the light was better, sat down and opened it. It contained a newspaper cutting. It described the caravan fire and the identification of the occupant, one Jake Bull. The death was being described as unexplained and under investigation. Bowen looked inside the envelope to see if it contained a note or letter. Nothing. He examined it and noted that there was no stamp or postmark, it had been hand delivered. His hands began to shake. He looked out of the window on to the street but couldn't see anyone loitering outside the apartment block. He walked over to his drinks cabinet to pour himself a drink. He was startled when his phone started to ring. He looked at it apprehensively for a few seconds before picking it up.

"Hello?"

"You have read the newspaper cutting, Bowen?"

It was Campeanu.

"Yes, I—"

"It was foolish of you to have employed a drunkard to help you with the burglary. A loose cannon that I could ill afford to be at large. You do understand?"

Bowen's heart began to beat too fast and sweat broke out on his brow.

"Yes, look, I'm sorry Campeanu, I was sure that he—"

"It's done now. I'll give you a chance to redeem yourself, Bowen. I have a little job for you. Get yourself down to Wales tomorrow. Don't drive, take the train. I'll meet you at the railway station in Towyn, the train should get in around seven in the evening."

Campeanu hung up before Bowen could reply. He held the phone in his hand, staring at it fearfully, as if he had just received his death sentence. He put it down slowly, took out his handkerchief and wiped his brow, trying to think of some way of extricating himself from the mess he was in.

A few minutes after Charles Bowen had taken a taxi to the station the next morning, the police called at his flat. They wanted to interview him about the fingerprints found on Gordon Bancroft's walking stick.

****

The old rectory where Reverend Anthony O'Malley lived was a large Victorian house, sadly neglected over the years. Largely un-modernised apart from having central heating installed, it was difficult to heat, had draughty sash windows and ill-fitting doors. It was an open invitation for any burglar, in fact.

Charles Bowen had no difficulty breaking in. Breaking was hardly the word to use, so easy was it to force an unlocked downstairs sash window. What he was looking for would be most likely found in whichever room Reverend Anthony used as an office. Certainly it would be on the ground floor. It took him less than five minutes to locate a large oak twin-pedestal desk covered in papers and various pieces of office equipment – stapler, hole punch, letter opener, green-shaded desk lamp, manila files both open and closed, letters and bills and half written sermons. But what he was looking for was the briefcase described in the Bancroft testament that contained the location of the Daniels treasure. He opened every desk draw and cupboard without success. The tall bookcase was the last piece of furniture unexplored. Bowen stood looking at it, not knowing what to do next when he spotted the leather covered corner of what might be the very thing he was looking for peeking over the top of the bookcase, much too high up for him to reach. He looked around for some library steps but saw none. He pulled the captain's chair close from the desk up to the bookcase and stood carefully on the seat, hoping it wouldn't swivel round as he stood on it, and with his outstretched fingertips managed to move the briefcase out far enough for it to topple off, narrowly missing his shoulder before it hit the floor. His weight shifted as he tried to avoid it, causing the chair to swivel round and throw him off. His head struck the corner of the desk as he fell heavily. He lay unconscious on the carpet bleeding profusely.

It was some time before Campeanu realised that Bowen wasn't going to come out. He put on a pair of gloves and entered through the open sash window and searched the rooms until he came across Bowen. He was groaning, laying face down and was just coming to. Campeanu turned him over and sat him up, propping him up against the desk.

"Did you find it?" he asked. Bowen nodded.

"Where is it?" Campeanu was casting about as he asked the question. Then he saw the briefcase lying underneath the desk. He picked it up and tried to open it but it had combination locks on each catch. He cursed and put the briefcase down. Bowen was still groaning and holding the wound on his head.

"Let's sort you out now, shall we?" said Campeanu. He manoeuvred Bowen away from the desk slightly, and kneeling behind him, he put his left arm around Bowen's face, one hand covering his mouth, gripped his forehead with his right arm, put his knee firmly in Bowen's back and twisted his head violently, causing Bowen's neck to break with a sickening crack. His body slumped forward. Campeanu released him, moving his body to its original position after the fall from the chair.

His hands were now bloody and there was blood on his jacket where Bowen's head wound had rested.

Campeanu went to the kitchen and washed his hands, dabbing at the blood on his clothing with some kitchen roll that he then put in his pocket. He went back to the study and surveyed the scene, picked up the briefcase and examined the locks. It was a cheap vinyl covered model. He smiled to himself. He put his ear to the first lock, moving the combination numbers slowly until he heard each one click, signifying that it had found its opening position. The lock sprung open. He repeated the operation on the second lock. It took time, too much time in his estimation. He was fearful that the Reverend Anthony would return before he had completed the job in hand. At last the second lock sprung open. He opened the case and found the letter that gave him the whereabouts of the bank in which the treasure was situated. He smiled to himself and wrote down the details with one of the pens on the desk, placed the letter back in the briefcase and shut it, revolving the combination numbers to lock it again. He pushed it back under the desk where he'd found it and surveyed the room again to make sure that there was nothing to suggest his presence at the scene. He walked out of the room and back out through the sash window, making sure that none of his footprints were visible outside on the drive. Now he faced the difficult task of somehow getting Lloyd and Asil Daniels to accompany him to the bank in question.

****

Reverend Anthony O'Malley returned later that afternoon, hung up his jacket and went through to his office. He was shocked to find a body lying in a pool of blood on the floor. He rushed over and felt for a pulse in the man's neck, but already knew by the coldness of his skin that he had been dead for some time. He saw the briefcase under the desk, looked at the overturned captain's chair and guessed what had occurred. He examined the briefcase. He was relieved to find that it had not apparently been opened. Nevertheless, he opened it and checked that all the papers were indeed still there. He picked up the phone and dialled John Nolloths number.

"John, I've discovered a dead body in the rectory. Can you come over before I call the police? I'm certain that it's to do with the Daniels inheritance."

Nolloth arrived within the hour. He examined the scene from all angles and stood rubbing his chin.

"You've not touched anything, Anthony?"

"Only the briefcase to check that nothing's missing."

"Good. Let's see what's in his pockets, shall we."

He found the usual things, wallet, driving licence, coins, keys, etc. He opened the wallet. It contained two credit cards, a debit card and notes to the value of seventy pounds. The driving licence clearly identified him as Charles Bowen.

"Charles Bowen, I know quite a bit about this man, Anthony. And you're quite right, he's been after information about Bill Daniels will, or rather *was*. You say nothing's missing from the briefcase?"

"No, nothing. It has combination locks. They're undamaged, and anyway, assuming that he fell while dislodging it from on top of the bookcase, I'd say that he didn't have any chance to get inside it."

"How did he get in, do you know?"

"The sash window in the drawing room. None of the windows have locks I'm afraid John."

Nolloth shook his head and tutted. "The police won't be happy about that you know, Anthony. Anyway, thanks for calling me first. You better call them now. It's best if you tell them that I was with you when you found the body and that it was me who emptied his pockets. Otherwise my fingerprints might confuse them. I'd better go before they get here. Call me on my mobile as soon as they've gone. No doubt they'll be in touch with me soon enough, although it looks like an accident so they shouldn't be too long in clearing this up."

"John, I can't thank you enough for coming over so quickly. You can't imagine what a shock it was to find that body in my office. I'll let you know what happens later. By the way, how is Asil? This business must be a terrible shock for the poor girl."

"She's coping remarkably well, Anthony. She's formed a strong friendship with a local man, Luke Lomax, who's helping her through this. She's a very strong character, thankfully. Her father didn't do her any favours with his dodgy dealings."

"No, but he was basically a good man. Give her my love won't you. And tell her that I'll be praying for her."

As soon as Nolloth arrived home he rang Arbelov to tell him what had happened.

"Are you quite sure that Bowen was alone John?"

"Fairly certain, yes. Well, it certainly looked like an accident. Although I'd be surprised if Campeanu wasn't involved somewhere along the line."

"Oh, without a doubt. Look John, this confirms just how determined Campeanu is. You better get O'Malley to find a safer place to keep that briefcase, Campeanu won't let it rest at that I'm sure. I think we better get back down to Suffolk. Can you make it down tomorrow? We could stay at Hintlesham Hall, if that's alright with you."

"Better that I leave now, before the police come calling after seeing Anthony."

"No, that's no good John. It's better that you see the police as soon as possible. They may suspect something if they think you're running away. See you tomorrow, eh?"

"Sure, if you think that's best."

****

Campeanu arrived back at the cabin in the woods. He unlocked the bar across the door and entered. Lloyd looked up apprehensively from the chair in which he was tied. Campeanu smiled as he approached him.

"It's alright, Lloyd, I've come to set you free. You see, I have a task for you."

He removed the tape over Lloyd's mouth and untied his hands. Lloyd rubbed his wrists vigorously to restore the flow of blood.

"Here, eat this. And here's a bottle of mineral water." He passed him a pack of sandwiches purchased from the garage where he'd filled the car with fuel. Lloyd drank some water and then set about eating hungrily.

"Now, I want you to send a message to your wife saying that you've been called away on urgent business and will contact her later tomorrow evening. Text it from your mobile, I know you have it with you. Do it now."

Lloyd retrieved his phone from his inside pocket, opened it and started to type a message.

"Let me see before you send it, Lloyd."

When he'd finished typing he showed it to Campeanu.

"Right, well done, Lloyd. You'll be quite safe while you do exactly as you're told. Now we're going to London. To the bank that holds the Daniel's items that interest me. Oh yes, Lloyd, I have the information. And yes, I found it in a briefcase at the old rectory where the Reverend O'Malley had it for safe keeping." Campeanu laughed at Lloyd's expression of incredulity.

"It's alright, Lloyd, he hasn't been harmed. You see, I get what I want. You are going to help me to convince the bank that we need to inspect the items they hold. If you fail to behave properly during this operation your dear wife might… Well, let's not go into that. Stand up, get your legs working and then we must start our journey."

Lloyd stood up and rubbed his knees and stamped his feet to get the circulation going again. Campeanu ushered Lloyd outside and into the car, not now worried that Lloyd would attempt to get away. He was much too frightened for that.

They arrived at an apartment adjacent to the one that Bowen occupied in Oakley Gardens, Chelsea. It was on the first floor overlooking the street. Campeanu showed Lloyd the bathroom and invited him to shower or whatever he wanted to do.

"We shall be staying here for the night, Lloyd. Please don't try anything; I don't want to use any violence. I promise you that as soon as I have the information I'm looking for at the bank, I will release you unharmed. Do I have your assurance?"

Lloyd nodded. "Yes. Yes, I promise." He couldn't really see what he could do, but he hoped that an opportunity would arise for him to either attract attention somehow or perhaps escape. He knew that this man, whoever he was, would show him no mercy if he were caught.

Campeanu pulled a chair over to the window where he could watch the street outside while Lloyd tended to his ablutions. Lloyd emerged from the bathroom and took a seat in one of the plush armchairs. Campeanu offered him a whisky and soda that Lloyd gladly accepted.

"I've ordered a couple of pizzas. I hope you like pizza? They should arrive any minute. We'll have a bottle of wine to drink with them."

About a half an hour later the pizzas duly arrived. Campeanu produced cutlery and two trays with warmed plates, salt and pepper mills and wine glasses. He opened a bottle of Valpolicella and poured it.

"Please start, Lloyd. It's all we'll be having before we travel to Suffolk early in the morning."

Before they had finished eating, Campeanu got up hurriedly and went over to the window. He looked out onto the street below and saw two police cars parked outside the entrance to the apartments. He could hear the policemen mounting the stairs to Bowen's apartment. It wasn't long before they departed, only to return a few minutes later. Campeanu assumed that they had needed to enlist the help of the caretaker to get the keys to the apartment. He signalled Lloyd to keep quiet and listened as he heard the police banging about next door. They were searching the flat and it took some time. They left eventually and Campeanu watched from the window as they drove away.

****

Nolloth met Arbelov as planned the next morning at the Hintlesham Hall Hotel in time for lunch.

"Any news?" Arbelov asked.

"Oh yes, the police were on to me last night. Rev Anthony O'Malley told them that I'd been at the scene. I got a right dressing down for interfering with the evidence. They kept me under interview for two and a half hours before I convinced them that I had nothing to do with the crime. They wouldn't let me go until they'd found out where Bowen lived; and when they realised that he'd travelled up from London they seemed to lose interest. They're not a very bright lot. I assume that they notified the Met to have his place searched. Do you think they'll find anything at his apartment?"

Arbelov laughed. "No, I don't think so, John. I had the pleasure of going over his place as soon as he left for Wales. I had no idea that he was going to his death, though. I didn't find anything of interest. Although I think his phone records might be revealing. I'm waiting to receive a list of his most recent calls. They're going to fax them to me here later today."

"So, are we any nearer to finding this Campeanu character?"

"Maybe the phone records will throw some light on that. Look John, I think you better get back to Towyn after all. The police might be suspicious to learn that you've gone away."

"So why did I have to drive all the way down here for a chat? We could have discussed this over the phone," said Nolloth irritably.

"I was hoping that by the time you got here I would have a change of plan. Not so. Sorry John. I'll carry on here and see if I can trace Campeanu. Keep in touch with the police in Towyn and ring me if anything develops."

Nolloth shook his head and sighed, showing his annoyance at the wasted journey. Arbelov had his reasons he was sure, but he obviously wasn't going to share them with him.

****

Asil and Luke were enjoying each other's company, so much so that they had put thoughts of any impending danger to the back of their minds. They attended the concert at the Regent Theatre in Ipswich. Asil was ecstatic over the performance; the whole programme consisted of modern works that she liked. She was familiar with Rachmaninov's *Second Piano Concerto* and loved it; and she found Barber's *Adagio for Strings* achingly beautiful. Luke wasn't that much into classical music but had to admit that he found it more interesting and enjoyable than he'd anticipated, especially Copland's *Appalachian Spring* that contained elements of jazz that intrigued him.

After the concert they went to the Chinese restaurant adjacent to the theatre and lingered over the meal, full of talk about the performance they'd just witnessed.

They were quiet on the drive home to Monks Eleigh, just content with being in each other's company. Asil part-reclined her seat, put on a Chet Baker CD, shut her eyes and let his silky voice caress the words of *My Funny Valentine*. Luke looked at her and smiled, aware of how strong his feelings for her were becoming and blessing the day that they'd met. He just wished that this wretched inheritance didn't exist and that they could forget about the danger that it might bring to them.

They were surprised to see that the lights were on in the house when they arrived home. It was just past midnight. Usually Mrs Wade and Belynda would have been in bed by that hour. An agitated Mrs Wade met them at the door and peered past them into the darkness outside.

"Isn't Mahari with you?" she asked.

"No, why would he be?" asked Asil, alarmed at the question.

"Oh, Asil, he's disappeared." She was frantic now, tears beginning to well up in her eyes. "I just hoped that somehow he would be with you. He went out for a walk about seven this evening, after we'd eaten, and never came back. I didn't know what to do. I didn't want to spoil your evening by phoning you. Should I have called the police do you think?"

"Now calm down for a minute Auntie, come and sit down." Asil put her arm around her and led her into the drawing room and sat her down in an armchair.

"What was he wearing? Did he take anything with him? He usually doesn't go far, there must be a logical explanation. Luke, what do you think?"

Marjorie Wade was crying openly now, holding her face in her hands with a tissue pressed to her eyes. Belynda sat on the arm of her mother's chair comforting her.

Belynda said, "He was just dressed in shirt, light pullover and jeans. Just as he always did when he went out for a walk."

Luke said: "Have you looked in his room? Did he leave a note?"

"Yes, we've looked, but no, no note."

"Have you tried the pub?"

Mrs Wade nodded.

Asil and Luke exchanged glances.

"Stay here Asil, I'll take the car and have a drive around the village."

Asil said, "I think we'll wait till the morning before we ring the police, just in case he turns up. I'm sure he will. Belynda, why don't you and your mum go to bed, it's very late and there's nothing you can do. I'll wait up for Luke. Go on, please."

"I shan't sleep a wink, I know I won't," said a still tearful Mrs Wade.

It was an hour and a half before Luke returned.

"I've looked everywhere Asil, even in ditches to see if he might have had a fall. The moon is as bright as day out there. No sign I'm afraid."

He hugged Asil and they clung together for a few seconds.

"He's been abducted, hasn't he, Luke. I just know it, I can feel it."

Asil was quite distraught.

"Now, now, Asil. Let's not jump to conclusions. Come on, let's get to bed and try to get some sleep. There really isn't anything more we can do tonight. In the morning I'll ask around to see if anyone saw him on his walk. Now we better phone John Nolloth and get his advice."

Nolloth was not answering his home phone or his mobile. They would have to wait until the morning.

****

Lloyd remained apprehensive about his future. He could see no prospect of escaping on the drive down to Suffolk. He imagined that the next destination would be to Asil Daniels' house. It would be impossible to access the bank vault in London without both Asil's and his own presence, so he felt reasonably safe for the time being. But after this man had whatever it was he wanted from the contents of the vault, what use would either Asil or he be? He shuddered to think of what fate had in store. This man was ruthless and he was certain that he wouldn't hesitate in getting rid of both of them if he thought they were a threat.

The car turned off the main road onto a narrow country lane. After a couple of miles it left the road and proceeded down a rough cart track and stopped outside a small thatched cottage. Once inside, Campeanu apologised before again binding Lloyd's legs and arms and tying him securely to a heavy oak upholstered chair.

"I'm so sorry, Lloyd, but I have to leave you for a few hours. I should be back by tonight. No one will bother you here, it's miles from the nearest house and no one comes along the track. I'll bring some food and something to drink for you when I return."

Campeanu drove to Ipswich and stopped at the Tesco superstore on the A12 Copdock interchange. He parked the car, bought a newspaper and settled himself in the restaurant to linger over a meal of bacon egg and chips. Afterwards, he purchased sandwiches and bottles of mineral water that he put in the boot of the car before heading for Monks Eleigh.

MAHARI

Mahari always looked forward to his evening walk. The whole ambience of the Suffolk countryside was so very different to that of his home in Wales. He never wanted to go back there now that Gordon Bancroft was dead. He knew that Asil and the Wades were doing their best to make him feel at home here but he felt that he was imposing on them. It might be that he would feel differently if he had his own place to live. As he wandered around the village, he tried to imagine what sort of place he would like to live in; cottage, house, converted barn, bungalow? Whatever he chose, it would have to be in good condition, he was not good at doing anything practical in the way of renovation. He was surprised that there didn't seem to be any 'For Sale' notices on any of the properties in the village.

It worried him that it might be difficult to find something near Asil, he wouldn't want to have to live miles away in Hadleigh or any of the other towns or villages.

A car pulled up a few yards in front of him and a man got out and walked towards him. He stopped and asked Mahari if he could tell him how to get to Bildeston. Mahari smiled and pointed to his own mouth and shrugged his shoulders. The man said, "Oh, I see, you can't speak?" Mahari nodded. "Then perhaps you would point it out on my map in the car?" Mahari nodded yes and followed the man back to the car. The man opened the passenger door, picked up a map from the seat, gave it to Mahari and ushered him in and shut the door. He then got in the drivers seat. He started the engine and began to drive off. Mahari began to panic and took hold of the man's arm to signal him to stop. "It's alright Mahari, don't worry. You see, I know who you are. You are going to accompany me on a little mission; I have something to show you. It's to do with your friend Asil Daniels. We don't have far to go so just keep calm and relax."

Mahari was inwardly fearful but there didn't seem that there was much he could do. He certainly didn't fancy his chances of jumping out of a moving car, and anyway, the man seemed quite friendly.

It was about half an hour before the car turned off the road and down a cart track. It stopped outside an isolated cottage. "OK Mahari, come with me, there's someone I'd like you to meet inside."

Mahari couldn't even guess who it might be.

It was nine o'clock when Lloyd heard the car draw up outside. He heard the door bang shut, then another door shutting. It must be two people, then? The door of the cottage opened and to Lloyds great surprise, a wide-eyed Mahari Artaxis was pushed in, with Campeanu following. On seeing Lloyd bound, Mahari started to back away towards the door. Campeanu pinned his arms behind him and manhandled him into a chair a few feet from Lloyd, where he was quickly bound to it.

Campeanu stood back to admire his work.

"Now isn't this cosy gentlemen? I must say that you have both behaved impeccably so far. I do hope that you will keep it up, otherwise it could be very unpleasant for you both."

He went out to the car and returned with a carrier bag full of sandwiches and bottles of mineral water.

"Now I'm going to untie your hands so that you can eat and drink."

Mahari refused to eat but drank some water. Lloyd ate and drank, making the food last as long as he could. They were both bound again when Lloyd had finished eating.

Campeanu's mobile rang. He answered it and spoke in his native tongue for a few seconds. He appeared agitated and paced the room while listening to whoever was on the other end of the line. Shaking his head he looked over to both Lloyd and Mahari and then shouted something incomprehensible down the phone. He cursed and kicked a waste paper basket across the room. He took the remaining sandwiches and water bottles and put them back in the carrier bag, looked around the room and went out without saying a word, slammed and locked the outside door after him. They heard the car start up and drive away at speed, wheels spinning. It was getting dark now, probably around ten o'clock Lloyd guessed. *What now?* he thought.

It was several hours later when they heard a car draw up outside. They were both filled with apprehension as to what sort of mood their abductor would be in. Instead of hearing the key in the lock, they heard the door being rattled and then silence. A few minutes later the lock on the door was being attacked. The sound of splintering wood was music to their ears. After quite a struggle, the door succumbed and a tentative Arbelov cautiously entered with gun in hand.

"Good God! Lloyd, Mahari! Are either of you hurt?" They both shook their heads.

"I can't tell you how relieved we are to see you, Arbelov."

Arbelov got to work setting them both free of their bonds.

"Who brought you here?" Arbelov asked Lloyd.

"He didn't tell me his name. Foreign, well built, eastern European…"

"Campeanu. It was a man called Campeanu, Romanian. A very dangerous man, you are very fortunate not to have suffered any harm. Do you know where he's gone? Did he say anything?"

"No, nothing. He answered a call on his mobile, got very agitated and drove off like a bat out of hell."

"OK, let's get you in the car and out of here before he comes back."

****

Asil couldn't sleep and tossed and turned before finally getting up at 5.30 in the morning. She couldn't wait any longer to phone John Nolloth. He was in bed fast asleep when he received Asil's call.

"John, I'm so sorry to get you out of bed so early. But we're so concerned about Mahari."

Nolloth tried to shake himself awake and absorb the information that Asil was giving him. He was very concerned when he heard the news about Mahari but tried not to appear too worried.

"You better inform the police about Mahari, there's not much I can do from here. I have some other information for you, Asil. Someone reported seeing a man escorting Jake Bull from the pub on the night he was killed. And it could well have been Campeanu."

"What does it mean, John?"

"I don't know. Jake Bull's death might be unconnected with Campeanu but I can't see it. I'll keep working on it from here. Unfortunately, I was down in Suffolk yesterday meeting Arbelov so I don't particularly want to drive back down again today. Have you heard from Arbelov?"

"No, not a word. I've tried his mobile but it's not switched on. I'm sure he'll ring though."

"Look, Asil, I'd better come down to see you, but not today. I'll be with you first thing in the morning and we can see what can be done. Yes, you'd better call the police now, don't waste any more time."

"Ok, I'll do that John, that's wonderful. Can't wait to see you."

Asil had just put the phone down from speaking to Nolloth when it rang before she could phone the police. It was Arbelov.

"Thank goodness you've phoned," said a relieved Asil. She told him about Mahari going missing the night before but was cut off in mid sentence.

"It's alright, Asil. I've located Mahari and I'm with him at this very moment. Asil, I can't explain on the phone. We will be with you in a couple of hours. You'd better prepare for a trip to London while you're waiting for us to arrive, I'll explain everything when we get to you."

Before Asil could say a word, Arbelov hung up. She ran back upstairs and into Luke's room, shaking him awake, and with tears in her eyes. She said: "He's safe. Mahari's safe, Luke, and Arbelov's on his way here with him. He says that we've got to leave for London as soon as he gets here!"

"How on earth did he find him? What did he say?"

"He'll tell us all about it when he arrives. Come on Luke, he'll be here in a couple of hours. You'll have to get dressed and ready for when they get here. It must be to the bank, mustn't it?"

Luke said irritably, "Asil, I've just woken up, I have no idea." He caught Asil's hand and pulled her towards him. "We've got half an hour Asil," he said sleepily, "hop into bed with me for a quick cuddle?"

She laughed, punched him hard on the shoulder and said: "Luke Lomax, you're impossible! Now get up and get dressed, please." She went quickly out of the room and back downstairs smiling to herself. It was such a relief to know that Mahari was safe. She made a pot of strong coffee and some toast for when Luke came down. They would need it if they were going to go straight to London.

It had started to rain heavily. Asil and Luke grabbed coats and waited for Arbelov to arrive. Meanwhile, she phoned Nolloth's mobile but he wasn't answering. She left a message and told him the news and that they would shortly be on their way to London and that they would speak again as soon as Arbelov arrived.

It wasn't long before they heard Arbelov's car splashing up the drive. He let a delighted Mahari out of the car. He looked dishevelled and pale. Asil ran down to the car to welcome him. Arbelov said abruptly, "Are you ready, Asil. We ought to leave at once. I'll explain in the car. I have another surprise for you. Walter Lloyd is in the car."

"*What!* How did he…?"

Arbelov opened the rear door, ushered Asil in beside Lloyd, and said, "Sorry Luke, you'll have to stay here. Look after Mahari; he's in shock at the moment. I'll ring you as soon as we get to London."

Luke was taken aback. "No chance, Arbelov, I'm not deserting Asil now. Mrs Wade can look after Mahari," he said, and settled himself in the front passenger seat.

Arbelov stood for a moment looking furious, then turned to Mahari, shrugged an apology, and got in the car.

"How on earth did you find them?" asked Asil.

"They were both abducted by Campeanu. I put a trace on Campeanu's phone, that's how I found them, holed up in a remote cottage down by the River Stour. Unfortunately, Campeanu had flown, on his way to the bank in London no doubt. That's why we must try and get there before he gets his hands on whatever it is that's in the vaults. He was going to get you, too, Asil, so that he could gain entry to the bank vault with Lloyd's help and a copy of the will. He forced Lloyd here to hand it over."

Lloyd said, "I'm so sorry, Miss Daniels. This Campeanu is a ruthless man and I'm no hero. It was all done at gunpoint. I'm just pleased to get out of the situation alive."

Asil clasped his hand and squeezed it. “Don’t worry Mr Lloyd, it’s not your fault. At least you and Mahari are safe, that’s what really matters most.”

Arbelov sat in the driver’s seat for a few seconds more, deep in thought.

“Change of plans. Lloyd, you better stay here with Mrs Wade and Mahari. You can get a taxi to run you into Ipswich in the morning. You can get a train to Towyn then. Your wife will be worried about you and we don’t really need you for us to access the bank. Is that OK?”

Lloyd thought for a moment. “Yes, that makes sense. I wouldn’t want Tamsin to be unduly concerned. Will you keep me in the picture please?”

“Of course. Now we really must go.”

Lloyd got out of the car and Arbelov left with the wheels of the car spewing wet shingle behind as he accelerated out of the drive.

Lloyd made his way up to the house. Mrs Wade had been standing at the door in her dressing gown. She welcomed a bemused Mahari back with a hug, and ushered him and Lloyd into the house. Tea was made and biscuits and cake offered with the promise of a proper meal to follow. Lloyd asked if he might ring his wife so Mrs Wade let him use the phone in the drawing room while she, Mahari and Belynda tucked into the tea and biscuits.

Lloyd’s wife Tamsin answered the phone after several rings and was surprised to hear her husband’s voice. He almost never rang her at this time of the morning.

“How are you, darling?” he asked.

She smiled. “Walter, have you phoned me at this hour just to ask how I am?”

“No, darling, of course not. But I’ve had rather a disturbing time. Will you be home on time tonight?”

"As far as I know, yes. Whatever's happened, Walter?"

He didn't reveal just what had happened to him in the last 48 hours, but she detected in his voice a note that was disturbing her.

"Look, I'll tell you all about it when you get home. I'll get a take-away for us and we can chat over that. Don't worry, darling, I'm alright now."

Lloyd joined Mahari and the Wades and began to tell Mrs Wade how he had been abducted and put in fear of his life.

Arbelov drove faster than his passengers felt comfortable with on the journey through Suffolk.

"Asil, I have some more disturbing news for you. After your uncle's body was exhumed, the pathologist was able to confirm that he had been injected with a lethal substance that caused his heart failure. As I'm sure you have already guessed, it was murder."

"How on earth was it missed by the coroner?" asked Asil.

"The coroner knew your uncle socially apparently. He knew that Bancroft had heart problems so his examination was cursory. He missed the puncture mark on his upper arm."

"They must have watched him die. It was Bowen, wasn't it? And Campeanu?" Asil shuddered at the thought. Luke held her hand tightly.

Arbelov said, "Yes, it was definitely Bowen and probably Campeanu as well, although we can't prove that at the moment. We have Bowen's finger prints on your uncle's walking stick though."

Asil remained quiet then. Arbelov concentrated on his driving and Luke held his hand out to Asil.

Once on the A12 dual carriageway, he maintained a steady 85 miles an hour, the car left a plume of spray behind them. Once in London Arbelov drove aggressively, swapping lanes and undertaking, flashing his headlights and sounding his horn when other vehicles got in his way.

****

Campeanu was furious. The mobile phone call he'd taken was from Romania. He had been told to pick up a colleague, superior in rank, from Stansted Airport immediately. His bosses obviously didn't trust him to bring this operation to a satisfactory conclusion on his own. He drove recklessly; well aware that time was of the essence. He was desperately trying to work out what he was going to do to get back to his two captives and get them to the bank. Once at the airport, time spent trying to find a parking space irritated him even more. He dared not risk having his car clamped for illegal parking.

He wasn't pleased when it was announced that the plane would be two hours late. He decided to get himself some breakfast while he waited, furious that so much time was being wasted. When the plane did finally arrive it was another 45 minutes before Valentin Neagu emerged in arrivals. Campeanu had worked with him before; there was no love lost between them. Neagu was more of a diplomat than he, not so ruthless but with an aggressively ambitious attitude. He was stocky, powerfully built, with short dark curly hair that made him look younger than his 43 years. He shook Campeanu's hand warmly enough, then both of them made their way hurriedly out to the car park. No word was spoken until they got in the car. Neagu was the first to speak.

"Ion, I know that we didn't hit it off on our last mission together. Let's forget that and start again, eh?"

Campeanu nodded agreement although he didn't expect to like Neagu any the better. Neagu continued: "I don't need to tell you that we must complete this operation quickly and efficiently. Bring me right up to date."

Campeanu briefed him up to the minute and told him that they were heading straight back to pick up Lloyd and Mahari. Neagu said, "Oh no, Ion, we go straight to the bank where the microfilm and codes are being held." Campeanu pointed out that he doubted whether they would get to the bank before Arbelov, as too much valuable time had been wasted due to having to divert to the airport. Neagu smiled. "You still bear a grudge, don't you, Ion? It was not my decision to have to help you on this case. And there was no way that I could have got here earlier. If we are too late, then we will have to revise our plans. But until then, let's hope that we will be in time, eh? We'll deal with your two captives later if we have to."

Campeanu drove more sensibly on the way to London. Fortunately the traffic was light and they made good progress. But he almost hoped that they would be too late and that then Neagu would be responsible for their failure.

THE BANK

When Arbelov, Luke and Asil arrived at the bank they were pleased that nobody had tried to contact the bank during the day prior to their arrival, so either Campeanu had given up for some reason or had a different plan yet to be revealed.

Asil and Luke threw their unworn coats onto a chair by the counter.

Arbelov asked one of the staff to get the manager, and was introduced to a Mr Tomlin. Arbelov presented him with all the necessary credentials to enable them access to the vault and the items contained within. A member of the bank staff led them down to the massive vault and went through the security procedure to open it. Asil was able to see once more all the unsold articles that she had last seen ten years previously, at the auction.

"What are we looking for, Arbelov?"

"I don't know, Luke. Just look at everything, see if there are any hidden documents."

Luke and Arbelov looked in vases, drawers in the few pieces of furniture, and examined pictures and photograph frames. Suddenly Arbelov pulled his mobile phone out of his pocket and tried to dial. He looked at the bank official. "No reception down here?"

"I'm afraid not sir," he said.

"Asil, something has just occurred to me. I must make a call. I'll be back in a couple of minutes."

Arbelov rushed up the stairs into the bank on the pretence of making a call on his mobile. He wasn't exactly sure what it was he had found taped into the back of the painting. He was sure that nobody had seen him remove it, and he was desperate to find out exactly what it contained. But he couldn't examine it in front of the others. He moved out into the street and headed for his car. Once inside he took out the small flat packet and unwrapped it. It wasn't a surprise to find that it was indeed a piece of microfilm. Attached to it was a square of thin but durable paper. He unfolded it and saw that it contained several patterns made up of figures and letters, probably 300-odd digits in total. It was some kind of code that didn't immediately convey anything to him. He needed time to work on it. Just as he was about to get out of the car and return to the bank a car pulled up slowly close behind his and a man got out. He recognised the man as Campeanu. Arbelov started the engine, put it into gear and floored the accelerator, rocketing off with wheels screaming. Campeanu was quickly back in his car and off in pursuit. Arbelov turned into Charing Cross Road, down to the Strand and along the Victoria Embankment at high speed, eventually turning off through Blackfriars underpass. After another couple of turns, eyes constantly scanning the rear view mirror, he took a left turn but finished up abruptly in a cul-de-sac. He punched the steering wheel in frustration, not convinced that he had lost Campeanu. Arbelov took out his mobile phone and rang Asil. No connection. He assumed that they were still in the vaults and unable to receive a signal. He turned the car around and stopped so that he could see any vehicle that might enter the cul-de-sac. He phoned John Nolloth and this time was relieved when he answered.

"Arbelov? What's going on? No ones mobiles are switched on! I've been—"

"Quiet, John. We've been in the vaults at the bank, so no reception. Now just listen carefully. I'm parked in – just a minute – Morgan's Lane, just off the embankment opposite HMS Belfast. I've found the microfilm that Campeanu is after and he's hot on my tail. I need to get it to you so you can get it analysed. Where are you?"

"I'm on the A406, just passing London City airport. Should be with you in about, say, 20 minutes?"

"Great. Providing Campeanu doesn't find me before you get here. Wait a minute – there's a London Hilton hotel I passed back up the road. The Tower Bridge Hotel. I'll meet you there."

He went back along the Tooley Road and into the hotel car park. He carefully parked the car so that it wasn't visible from the entrance and walked into the lounge and ordered himself a coffee.

****

Luke looked puzzled, but kept searching. Asil hadn't bothered to keep looking, as she hadn't a clue as to what she was supposed to be looking for and she was concerned about Arbelov's sudden departure. The bank official looked at his watch.

"I'm afraid we will have to close the vault in another 15 minutes, Miss Daniels."

"Oh. Alright. Shouldn't Arbelov be back by now?" she asked Luke.

Luke looked at his watch. "He's been gone half an hour. He's probably upstairs, go and tell him we're running out of time Asil."

Arbelov was nowhere to be seen in the bank. She asked the clerk where Arbelov had gone.

"He rushed straight out into the street about half an hour ago."

Asil went outside and looked up and down the street. She walked the hundred yards or so to see if he was sitting in the car. No sign of him there and no sign of the car either.

She started to panic. Was he all he seemed to be? Had he been abducted? Surely he wasn't in it with Campeanu? Her mind was in a whirl. She ran back to the bank and down to the vault.

"He's gone, Luke," she said, breathlessly.

"Gone? What do you mean, gone?"

"He's nowhere to be seen. The car's gone too."

Luke thought for a moment. He went over to one of the paintings he had looked at earlier in the search. He tipped it forward and examined the back and stood staring at it.

"What a fool I've been, Asil. Look here." The back of the painting had been cut open. "It wasn't like that when I looked at it before Arbelov disappeared. I saw him handling it a moment before he tried to make that phone call."

"What are you saying, Luke? Surely Arbelov wouldn't—"

"Surely Arbelov would! I thought it odd when he asked the clerk about not getting a signal down here. He would have known that, surely. Come on Asil, we need to get hold of John Nolloth, and quickly."

STANDING AND FALLON

The Sekurias office was on the tenth floor, its floor to ceiling window overlooking a grey and dismal London City, the HSBC building towering above.

It was furnished with a stainless steel and glass topped table, white leather chairs, and a vast ivory coloured desk. A large picture of Barack Obama hung on the left hand wall, a Stars and Stripes American flag on the opposite wall.

The stainless steel nameplate on the desk identified its occupant as Todd A Roberts.

Roberts picked up the intercom and asked his secretary to send in the two men who had been waiting nervously in the outer office.

Roberts stood up as they entered the office and advanced towards them, arm extended to shake their hands warmly.

Matt Phillips and Grant Evans were directed to sit in the two white leather chairs. Both were ex SAS now working for this American security company. Sekurias recruited mercenaries to serve in their operations in Iraq, Pakistan and Afghanistan.

They were nervous because they assumed that they were going to be sent back to either Iraq or Afghanistan.

"Hey you guys, why such long faces? Is this an English thing?" Roberts said laughing. "Relax, I have a mission for you. And it's right here in your dear old London."

Phillips and Evans looked at each other and smiled.

"Now, that's better."

Roberts pushed two manila folders across the desk towards them.

“You’ll find all you need inside, gentlemen. Identity cards that say you are Special Branch officers. They aren’t particularly good, but good enough to fool the people that you’ll be meeting. You are now Geoffrey Standing and Gordon Fallon. Now, the task is simple. You have to retrieve a valuable piece of microfilm and some sheets of code from the people detailed in your folder. Don’t carry anything on you that can be used to track your true identity. You have no need to use force. But if it’s necessary, then do so, this mission is that important.”

Roberts paused and studied both men for a few seconds. “You *are* armed?” They nodded. “Follow the instructions in the folder. You’ll have to act quickly. Today. So go to it you Limeys, and *don’t* let me down, OK?”

Standing and Fallon, or rather Phillips and Grant, stood up, shook hands once again with Roberts and headed for the door, each clutching their manila folder.

****

The bank clerk locked the vault and followed Asil and Luke back up the stairs and into the bank. They were surprised to find two men barring their way. They waited for the bank clerk to lock the door behind him.

“Where’s Arbelov?” said one of the men abruptly.

“Arbelov’s gone, he left about three quarters of an hour ago,” said Luke.

“*Gone?* Gone where?”

The two men looked at each other.

“You better both come into the manager’s office,” said the taller of the two men.

“Who the hell do you think you are?” said Luke; furious at the way they had been spoken to.

They were ushered into the manager’s office.

"Sit down and shut up. My name's Standing and this is Mr Fallon." They both brandished identity cards too quickly for Asil or Luke to read, but enough to see that they were on government business.

"Now, what did you find down there?" Standing looked from one to the other. Asil and Luke exchanged glances.

A subdued Luke said, "We didn't find anything. We didn't know what we were supposed to be looking for. I think Arbelov found something, though. I noticed he'd taken something from the back of one of the paintings just before he disappeared."

Asil frowned and shot a disapproving look at Luke.

"And you didn't ask him what it was he'd found?"

"No. I didn't realise until after he'd gone. I'd looked at the painting before hand. I'd noticed him fiddling with it just before he tried to make a call on his mobile. That's when he rushed out saying he had an urgent call to make. He said he'd be back."

Standing asked Fallon to get the bank manager and take them all back into the vault.

Once inside, Standing asked Luke to point out the painting. Fallon examined the paper covering where it had been slit open.

"Nothing obvious, sir. Must have been quite small. Shall we take the painting, have it tested by forensics?"

Standing nodded. "Don't worry, we'll give you a receipt. Perhaps our chaps will be able to determine what was hidden inside it. My guess is a piece of microfilm. What do you think, Fallon?"

"Couldn't be anything much bigger by the looks of it, sir."

The two men took a cursory glance at all the other items, then Standing asked the manager, Tomlin, to lock the vault and keep it locked. They all went back up into the bank.

"I'm afraid we need to ask you both a few questions. Have you got Arbelov's mobile number?"

Asil hesitated. She didn't want to betray Arbelov, but she wasn't sure now if he was on their side or not. "Yes. Here," she said reluctantly, writing his number down for him.

"You phone him," said Standing. "Ask him where he is and how long it will take him to get here. I wouldn't mention us if I were you. You are all under suspicion at the moment."

"What do you mean?" asked Luke, frowning and taking umbrage at the implication of the remark. "Under suspicion for what?"

"It's alright, Mr Lomax. Just remember that we've found you all here in the vaults of a bank with what could possibly be the nation's security at stake. Do either of you know Arbelov's background?"

Luke shook his head and fired a look at Asil.

"We don't know much about you, either, Mr Lomax. But we're going to find out all about everyone in due course. So just do as I say for the moment, OK?"

Luke looked enquiringly again at Asil. She shrugged acceptance of the situation.

"Now, Miss, please phone Arbelov and ask him the question."

Arbelov's mobile rang. He looked at the number before answering it and recognised Asil's number.

Asil pressed the phone tightly to her ear so that Standing wouldn't be able to hear Arbelov's voice.

"Asil, thank God. I've been trying to ring you. I expect you—"

"Where are you and how long will it take you to get here?"

Arbelov paused, recognising a tone in Asil's voice that rang alarm bells.

"Are you alone Asil? Just cough if you can't answer."

Asil coughed.

"I'll be there in about an hour, Asil," he said and then whispered: "John Nolloth will be here shortly," then hung up.

He sat down in the hotel lounge and waited for Nolloth. He feared that Campeanu had got to Asil and Luke. He needed time to think.

"Well, what did he say and where is he?" asked Standing impatiently.

"He said he'd be about an hour."

"And did he say where he was?"

"No. He hung up before I could ask him."

Standing looked at Fallon, sighed and raised his eyebrows.

Tomlin said, "I'm sorry, but how long do you think we have to stay closed? The staff need to know what's happening."

Standing said: "You'll stay closed for a while yet. We need your office until a colleague arrives, you see."

"If I have to stay closed, I need to notify head office."

"That won't be necessary Mr Tomlin. May I suggest that you send the staff home, this bank will remain closed for the rest of the day."

Once the staff had left, the manager locked the door.

"I'll have the keys, please," said Standing.

"Why?" asked Tomlin.

"I'll need to let my colleague in when he arrives and I want you to open the vault again. We need to have another look down there."

The manager gave him the keys to the door.

Standing said, "Come on, we'll all go down to the vault, you two can help me look again at the remaining paintings and see if there's anything else hidden. Fallon, you stay up here in case Arbelov arrives."

He gave Fallon the key to the door. Then he ushered all of them back down the stairs. Tomlin unlocked the vault and they all went in.

"Now I'll have the vault keys please."

"I'm sorry Mr Standing, but I'm not allowed to let anyone have these keys."

"We'll see about that," said Standing, snatching the keys from Tomlin's hand and making for the door. He went out quickly, closed and locked the door behind him.

Luke and Asil flinched at the sound of the door locking. The manager, Tomlin, stood incredulous with mouth agape.

Luke said in a hoarse voice: "What the hell's going on?"

Asil began to shake. The thought of being locked in the underground vault terrified her. Tomlin said, "Try not to worry Miss Daniels. If I fail to return home my wife will be taking some sort of action. She's always been fearful that someday I might be kidnapped and forced to hand over money or something. Silly I know, but…"

"It's alright Mr Tomlin. I'm sure Mr Arbelov will think of something. What do you make of Standing and Fallon, Luke?"

"I should have studied those identity cards more thoroughly. They looked official, though. It's my fault, Asil."

"Don't be silly, Luke, it's as much my fault as yours."

"It's not you're fault, either of you. If it's anyone's fault it's my staff that are to blame. They should have confirmed their identity. Unfortunately there's nothing we can do down here. No mobile phones work in the vault and that door is impregnable. I'm afraid we'll just have to wait and hope."

****

Nolloth parked his car in the hotel car park and hurried in to reception, spotting Arbelov drinking coffee in the lounge.

Arbelov stood up as soon as he saw Nolloth.

"Thank God you're here, John. Asil and Luke are at the bank and I think that maybe Campeanu has got to them. Asil sounded frightened on the phone and she confirmed that she couldn't talk. I've got what Campeanu was looking for. It appears to be a piece of microfilm and a coded piece of paper that will need deciphering. Any suggestions?"

Nolloth paused and rubbed his chin.

"What if I go to the bank and see what's going on? It might prove something and if Campeanu were alone, at least there would be three of us in there. And perhaps you could work something from outside?"

"Hmm, Campeanu is bound to be armed, John. It's a bit risky. No, this is what we'll do..."

Arbelov decided that he would use Nolloth's car to get to the bank, and to Nolloth's annoyance, decided that he would drive, as he knew London better. Arbelov drove as aggressively as he had done on the way from Monks Eleigh. Nolloth sat with fists clenched and eyes shut expecting to be involved in a crash at any moment.

****

Standing was getting tired of waiting for Arbelov. He paced up and down until Fallon said: "For God's sake, you're making me nervous. Arbelov must have sensed that something's wrong, maybe he won't—" Just then there was a knocking at the bank door. They both looked at each other. Standing said to Fallon, "Go and open it. I'll cover you. Stand behind the door when you've opened it." He drew his gun and stood well away from the door, facing it. Fallon opened the door slowly, hiding behind it. Very slowly, Arbelov moved into the foyer and was immediately confronted by Standing aiming a gun straight at him. He stopped dead and looked around, seeing Fallon behind him. Fallon shut and locked the door.

"Steady now, Arbelov. No sudden movements, right? Frisk him, Fallon." And to Arbelov he said, "Right, face the wall Arbelov. Spread your legs, hands above your head against the wall."

Arbelov did as he was told. He was puzzled. There was no sign of Campeanu and he had no idea who these men were. Fallon searched him thoroughly but found no weapon.

"He's clean. Shall I empty his pockets?" Standing nodded. Fallon went through every pocket placing the contents onto a small table.

"So, Arbelov. You know what it is we want. Where is it?"

"Where are Asil and Luke?"

"I'll ask the questions, Arbelov. If you want to see them alive you better give me an answer."

"I think I have you at a disadvantage. I have what you want. Before I give you any information I want to see Asil and Luke."

Standing looked at Fallon and back to Arbelov.

"Very well." He nodded to Fallon. "Go and fetch them."

Fallon went down to the vault and unlocked the door and opened it, gun at the ready. All three stood as far away from the door as they could get. "Come on you lot, out and up the stairs. I wouldn't advise you to try anything."

All three obeyed. The first person they saw when they emerged from the stairs was Arbelov. Asil's joy turned to horror when she saw Standing pointing a gun at him.

"Go and stand next to Arbelov you three. Now Arbelov, I want the goods you have. I'll give you no more time. I can put a bullet in Asil's knee-cap for starters to help you make up your mind." He pointed the gun at Asil's left knee.

"Well?"

"OK. The microfilm is hidden in the car outside. The car is a hundred yards down the road. Do I have your word that none of these three will be hurt if I give you the film?"

"You are in no position to make deals, Arbelov. The goods, then we'll talk." He turned to Fallon.

"Go with him and bring him back here with the goods. Be careful. Go."

Fallon waved the gun at the door and nodded to Arbelov to leave, following him closely with the gun in his coat pocket but pointed at Arbelov's back. He closed the door behind him and Standing locked it. Tomlin looked white and held his head in his hands. He subsided slowly onto his haunches. Asil said, "Couldn't we sit down please? We all need a drink of water."

Standing said, "Yes, sit. And no, you'll have to wait for a drink until Fallon gets back. I'm not letting any one of you out of my sight, understand?"

Tomlin said, "There is a water cooler behind the counter. Please I need to take a tablet."

Standing looked behind the counter. "Ok, you, Luke, get three cups of water. But do it slowly and within my sight."

Luke reluctantly did as he was told.

ESCAPE

They reached the car. Arbelov unlocked it with the remote and opened the passenger door.

"Wait. Where's the film?" asked Fallon.

"In the glove box."

"Stand back. I'll get it. You might have a gun in there for all I know."

Fallon slid into the passenger seat and opened the glove box. That was when Nolloth hit him, hard, with the butt of Arbelov's pistol. He fell forward and before he could react, Arbelov grabbed Fallon's gun from his pocket. Blood trickled from Fallon's head wound but he was conscious.

"Well done John! I don't think he'll give us much trouble now. Right Fallon, out!"

Fallon got out slowly and stood groggily by the door of the car, staunching the trickle of blood from the back of his head with his handkerchief. Nolloth was already out of the car and covering Fallon with Arbelov's gun.

"Now, Fallon, who are you two working for?"

Fallon sneered and said, "Get lost, Arbelov."

"Alright, let's go and see your partner, shall we? I'd co operate if I were you. Get moving."

Arbelov knocked on the door of the bank. Inside, Standing walked to the door and said, "Is that you, Fallon?"

Nolloth poked Fallon hard in the back with the gun. Fallon answered an affirmative. Standing walked away from the door and told Tomlin to go and open it. Fallon entered closely followed by Arbelov and Nolloth.

"You can drop that gun, whatever your name is." Standing looked from Arbelov to Nolloth, both pointing their guns at him. Nolloth ran to Standing's side and grabbed his gun while he was still trying to comprehend what was happening.

Arbelov said, "Mr. Tomlin, would you be so kind as to escort these two gentlemen to the vaults and lock them in? Mr Nolloth here will accompany you."

Tomlin retrieved the keys from Standing. The two went meekly down the stairs to the vault after being frisked for any more weapons and were duly locked in.

When Tomlin returned, Arbelov took him into the office and shut the door. He took ten minutes to talk to Tomlin. Nolloth saw through the window that Arbelov got Tomlin to sign something before they both re-emerged.

"Right, I think we can leave now, John. Mr Tomlin, please phone the police and report an armed robbery would you? I suggest that you wait here until they arrive. Come on Asil, let's get out of here before the fireworks begin."

Luke took Asil's hand and hurried out with Nolloth and Arbelov towards the car.

****

Tomlin heard a loud knocking at the bank door. To his great relief he thought the police had arrived in double quick time. As he opened the door it was thrust hard open, knocking him off his feet. Neagu thrust a gun into Tomlin's face, then fired two shots into the floor beside him. Tomlin cowered on the floor expecting to be killed. Instead, Neagu helped him up, looked around and led Tomlin into his own office and sat him in a chair. They heard another shot from outside the bank. Neagu stopped and looked puzzled, then continued.

"What's your name?" Neagu asked. Tomlin told him.

"Now, tell me what's been happening here, Tomlin. Every detail, you understand? And quickly, now."

Tomlin nervously related how Arbelov, Asil Daniels and Luke had arrived and searched the vault for something that he thought Arbelov had found and made off with. He explained how Standing and Fallon had taken over but were now locked in the vault, Arbelov having departed as Neagu had arrived.

"I presume that they are not armed?"

"No, Arbelov disarmed them both."

"OK, give me the keys to the vault."

Tomlin gave him the keys. "Lead the way, Tomlin."

Neagu knew that Tomlin wouldn't try anything. He looked drawn and resigned to whatever his fate would be. Not surprising with what had happened to him in the last few hours. When they had stepped down to the vault, Neagu gave Tomlin the keys and told him to unlock the door but not to open it. Neagu slowly pushed the door open and peered inside. Standing and Fallon were standing together at the back of the vault, not knowing what to expect.

Neagu walked in, covering them with his revolver.

"Keep your hands raised, please, gentlemen. So, tell me what exactly it is that you are you doing here?"

Standing explained that they were MI6 officers and reached for his inside pocket.

"Oh no, *don't* do that. Mr Tomlin here will look in your pockets."

He signalled Tomlin to do just that. Tomlin retrieved the identity cards and gave them to Neagu. He studied them and smiled.

"Do you think that these would fool anyone? I think you better tell me exactly who you are. And quickly, I am a very impatient man."

The two men looked at each other but remained silent.

"Very well, I'm sure that you have both watched gangster films. I'll count to five. Now: One two, three, four… I'm deadly serious, gentlemen." There was still no reaction from either man. Neagu had deduced that Standing was the more senior of the two. He pointed the revolver at Fallon's thigh and fired. Fallon screamed and fell to the floor, clutching his thigh. Tomlin retreated to the far side of the vault and faced the wall, his hands covering his eyes.

"Now, man, the truth, you're next."

"Ok, ok! We work for Sekurias, it's a—"

"I know who they are, man. These identity cards don't say who you really are. Tell me."

Standing told him their real names and that they were ex SAS and were employed by Sekurias as mercenaries.

Neagu retrieved the keys from a quaking Tomlin.

"You better put a tourniquet on your friend's leg, before he bleeds to death. Come on, Tomlin, let's get out of here."

Neagu locked the vault door and both men went back up into the bank where Neagu threw the keys to Tomlin and said, "Lock the door behind me and don't attempt to leave. The police should be here very soon. Once I've gone you can tell them anything you like."

He left and waited until he heard Tomlin lock the door. He looked for the car and Campeanu but both had disappeared. He hailed a taxi and asked to be taken to the Docklands railway station. He was heading to a pre-arranged rendezvous with Campeanu.

****

Nolloth asked as they were walking to the car, "What was going on between you and Tomlin?"

Arbelov smiled. "I was just making sure that he would give the police a story that wouldn't involve any of us actually being there when the attempted robbery took place. I invoked the official secrets act just to protect Asil. All we have to do now is get this microfilm analysed and hope that Campeanu doesn't show up again."

"Where are you taking it?"

"I'm going to post it— *What was that?*"

They all stopped. It sounded like muffled gunshots coming from the direction of the bank.

"The police couldn't have got there so soon, surely."

They still had 50 yards to cover before reaching the car just as they saw a figure leave the bank at a run towards them. They ran the last few yards to the car.

"Quick, get in!"

They piled into the car as a shot rang out and a side window of the car shattered. Luke uttered a soft groan and collapsed onto Asil, who screamed as she saw blood splattered over the seat. Arbelov pulled away with tyres screaming. Nolloth and Asil ducked out of sight. Luke had been hit and was bleeding profusely.

"Stop Arbelov. For Gods sake, *stop!* Luke's been hit!"

Arbelov took no notice until he'd put some distance between the car and the bank.

"Where the hell did Campeanu come from! It *was* him, wasn't it? I'll pull into the next side road, Asil. Where has Luke been hit?"

"It seems to be his left arm. I'll see if I can get a tourniquet on it when we stop. He's losing a lot of blood. We should get him to hospital John, and quickly."

Arbelov didn't bother to stop but headed straight for St Thomas's by Westminster Bridge. Asil tore a strip from Luke's shirt and made a tourniquet that she tied tightly around his upper arm. The bullet had passed right through. She was glad to see that it didn't look as if the bone had been shattered. She cradled Luke's head as he leaned against her, groaning with the pain. Asil was in tears.

Arbelov screeched to a halt outside A&E. He asked Nolloth to go and park the car and stay with it while they saw to Luke. He and Asil took Luke into A&E while Nolloth parked the car and stayed with it. As they got to reception Arbelov realised that he had left the microfilm in the car, but as Nolloth would be there he decided that he shouldn't be too concerned. He didn't expect that they would be long in the hospital.

Nolloth found a parking place as far away from other cars as he could, reclined the seat and opened the driver's window. He laid back and closed his eyes; glad to relax after such a hectic day. His thoughts wandered back to the time when Asil had been kidnapped in Thorpeness all those years ago. How brave that little girl had been, especially after what she'd been through after the death of her parents. Now she was going through yet another terrifying experience, being locked in a bank vault and seeing the man she obviously loves, shot at and injured. He'd spent 40 years in the police force and had seldom come across a case that had aroused so much anger in him. Tiredness overtook him and he drifted off to sleep.

Nolloth was awoken by the touch of cold steel pressing against his temple. Alarmed, he looked up to see the smiling face of Campeanu looking down at him, a revolver fitted with a long silencer pressed against his temple. Nolloth cursed himself for not being more vigilant.

"No sudden movements Mr Nolloth. I'll get in beside you." Campeanu walked to the other side of the car, the gun still trained on Nolloth, and slid into the passenger seat.

"Now, the film. I need it now. Where is it?"

"You expect me to tell you?"

"Well now, let's see. I can put a hole in somewhere painful for starters, followed by another one if you would be foolish enough not to tell me."

Campeanu felt in the door pockets while he was talking. Then he opened the glove compartment. His eyes lit up. "Well, what have we here? It seems that your kneecaps will remain intact Mr

Nolloth. How very foolish of Arbelov not to take better care of valuable property. Step out of the car now please." The smile had vanished and was replaced by a note of menace. Nolloth got out, followed by Campeanu. He beckoned Nolloth to the back of the car. "Open the boot and get in. But first, your mobile phone please, and your gun." Nolloth could see no way out of this. Knowing Campeanu, he knew that he would be lucky to get away with his life. He climbed into the boot and the lid shut with a loud clang. He heard Campeanu lock the car and walk away. He walked swiftly to his own car and rang Neagu to tell him that he had the microfilm. He drove off, heading for London City Airport and meeting up again with Neagu before leaving the country.

It was an hour before the duty doctor called Luke in for attention. Arbelov and Asil went with him. The doctor dealt quickly and efficiently with the wound without saying anything. When he had finished he said to Arbelov, "This is a gunshot wound. I will have to report it to the police I'm afraid and you will have to remain here until they arrive. Mr Lomax will need to stay here overnight, he's still suffering from shock and we have to be careful about any infection."

Arbelov pulled out his identity card and showed it to the doctor.

"I don't think that will be necessary, Doctor. This is a matter of national security. I'm sure you understand? I'll make sure that Mr Lomax is taken care of."

The doctor studied the identity card, made a note of the name and rank then said, "Mr Lomax will need strong pain killers and further attention from his own doctor as soon as possible." He wrote out a prescription and handed it to Arbelov. Arbelov thanked him and they left, Asil and Arbelov supporting a still unsteady Luke on each side. They spotted the car across the far side of the car park. On approach they heard a banging coming from the boot. Arbelov rushed to the car and tried to open it. He reached in through the shattered side window and pulled the door catch up, unlocking all the doors and the boot. A relieved Nolloth climbed stiffly out, rubbing his knees to get circulation back.

"What took you so long?" he said irritably.

"Never mind that, what's happened?"

Nolloth explained and apologised for not being more alert. Arbelov looked at his watch and guessed that Nolloth had been locked up for just over an hour. "Campeanu will be miles away by now. I suggest we go back to the Tower Hill Hotel and rest for a while." Asil installed Luke comfortably in the back seat and climbed in beside him. "It's no good sitting in the car, Asil, Campeanu took the keys and I don't have a spare set. Better order a taxi and I'll get the car picked up later."

The taxi arrived ten minutes later. It didn't take long to get to the hotel, where Arbelov booked an apartment and ordered coffee and sandwiches to be delivered up to them.

Asil took Luke into the bedroom of the apartment and made him lie down. He was still shivering from the shock. Arbelov asked Nolloth to go and fetch the painkillers while he made some phone calls. The first thing to do was to make sure all ports and airports were alerted to Campeanu, although he really knew that he was too clever to be caught now. He was furious with himself for underestimating Campeanu's ability to track them to the bank. His next call was to establish what had happened at the bank. The phone rang and was answered by a policeman. Arbelov stated who he was and asked to speak to the officer in charge.

"Please tell me what you've found," asked Arbelov. The officer insisted on getting security clearance before giving him any details. Arbelov gave him a number to ring, a person's name to speak to and told him to hurry up and get back to him.

The officer took 15 minutes to ring back.

"It's all a bit confusing, Mr Arbelov. The manager, a Mr. Tomlin, seems to be in a state of shock and isn't able to tell us anything coherent. He took us down to the vault where we discovered two men, one suffering from a gunshot wound. Neither of them will talk, not even to confirm their names. They are in possession of false identity cards, purporting to be MI6 officers. We're going to turn them over to the terrorist unit once a doctor has tended to the injured man. Tomlin says that it wasn't him who shot the man but refuses to say who did. We haven't found any firearms on the premises, either. That's about all I can tell you at the moment, I'm afraid sir."

"OK, that's fine, and thanks."

He went into the bedroom to find Luke asleep and Asil lying on top of the bed, propped up on one elbow and holding his hand.

"I'll book us in overnight here, Asil. John's gone to get the painkillers for Luke. We can have evening meals sent up to our rooms if you like. We'll leave for Monks Eleigh first thing in the morning. I think this little adventure is over for now."

Asil thanked him and said that would be fine. He walked out and closed the door behind him.

Ten minutes later John Nolloth knocked on the door and came into the room.

Luke had just woken up.

"Hello, you two young lovers," Nolloth said smiling. "Got some pain killers for you, Luke. Two every four hours, no more, right? How are you feeling?"

Luke answered weakly "A bit shaky still. It hurts like hell."

Asil thanked Nolloth for getting the painkillers.

"I've got to sort myself out a car and get back to Towyn now, Asil. I'll be in touch soon, though. Look after that man of yours, won't you." He blew her a kiss, waved goodbye to Luke and left.

Asil kissed Luke on the cheek.

"Of course I'll look after you. But you better behave yourself young man!"

Sleep came fitfully for Luke. When the painkillers wore off, Asil was there to make sure that he took another dose. By morning Luke was feeling much better, so they went down to the dining room for breakfast and were shortly joined by Arbelov. As he passed Asil's chair he stooped and kissed her on the forehead, then shook Luke's hand and sat down at the table.

"Are you feeling fit enough to travel, Luke?"

Asil had made a sling for Luke's arm but he was still looking very pale.

"I'll be fine. You'll have to convince nurse here, though!" he said smiling weakly at Asil.

"He can't even cut up his breakfast, I'm having to do it for him! But I'm not going to feed it to him," laughed Asil. "Yes, we'd like to get home as soon as we can. Are you sure that you can spare the time to drive us all the way back to Suffolk?"

"It's the least I can do after what you two have been through. Right then, we'll leave as soon as you two brave souls are ready, OK?"

It was an hour and a half though before they came down the stairs and into the reception area, where Arbelov was reading the morning paper and enjoying a cup of coffee. He finished his coffee and they made their way out to the car.

"Any sign of Campeanu and that other man?" asked Asil.

"None at all. We've failed miserably, but at least you two are safe, that's the important thing."

The painkillers put Luke to sleep on the rest of the journey; Asil was just content to have his head resting on her shoulder.

****

Mrs Wade was delighted and relieved when Arbelov's car pulled up outside the house in Monks Eleigh later that morning. As Luke got out of the car she spotted his arm in a sling and rushed to him, full of concern. "Whatever's happened to you two?"

"It's alright Aunt Marjorie, Luke's fine. We'll tell you all about it after we've had a nice cup of tea and something to eat, we're starving!" Asil winked at Luke and smiled. Arbelov followed them but stopped them at the door and said, "As much as I'd like a cup of tea, Mrs Wade, I really must get back to London. There's still much to do if we are going to catch Campeanu." He turned to Asil. "Please forgive me, Asil, I'm sure you understand." Asil embraced him and kissed him on both cheeks. "How can we thank you enough for what you've done? You know you'll be welcome here anytime. Please keep in touch, won't you?"

"I certainly will. Now I really must say goodbye."

He headed for his car and waved out of the window as he drove down the drive.

Mrs Wade made tea and Asil helped make sandwiches. They sat around the kitchen table while Asil related in great detail all that had befallen them since they'd left in the pouring rain in what seemed an age ago. After the tea and biscuits, Asil drove Luke to the doctor's and got him sorted out.

Later that afternoon she phoned John Nolloth and thanked him again for his help. Luke went home and told his mother every thing that had happened to them. He returned to Asil's later that evening.

A couple of days later Konstantin Arbelov informed them that Standing and Fallon, or rather Matt Phillips and Grant Evans, were now in custody awaiting trial. They had been working for an American security company based in London but operating in Iraq and Afghanistan. Ion Campeanu had hired a private executive jet from London City airport with a colleague, apparently heading for Schipol airport in Holland. No more news of either of them had been heard to date, although Arbelov seemed certain that the authorities would eventually catch up with them.

****

Asil and Luke discussed what to do with the contents of the bank vault in London. They had resolved to auction the remainder of all her inheritance and bank the money. She arranged the selling of Gordon Bancroft's old house for Mahari and they were both surprised at how much it fetched, it being of historical importance. Certainly more than enough to allow Mahari to buy a lovely 18th century Georgian house big enough for Mrs Wade and Belynda to move in and look after his needs, and within half a mile of Asil's house.

Asil and Luke decided to get engaged. Luke moved in with Asil and part of the triple garage was converted into a workshop so that Luke could carry on supplying his customers with specialised vintage and classic car parts once all his machinery had been transferred from his mother's garage. Asil acted as office manager and set up an office in the converted attic. She constructed a website for him and the business began rapidly taking off, enough for Luke to employ a good engineer to help with the workload.

Life was transformed for Asil. No longer the dark cloud of her inheritance hanging over her, no more bouts of depression, no more nightmares. Just a silver box that she kept under her pillow to remind her of her parents; and a life with a man that she was very much in love with.

THE END

www.ingramcontent.com/pod-product-compliance
Ingram Content Group UK Ltd.
Pitfield, Milton Keynes, MK11 3LW, UK
UKHW020415250726
13967UKWH00007B/2655